The Bull Rider's
Second Chance

THE BULL RIDER'S SECOND CHANCE

A RODEO ROMEOS ROMANCE

LEAH VALE

TULE
PUBLISHING

CHAPTER ONE

"EXCUSE ME."

Bodie Hadley heard the female voice over the pre-parade commotion and hoped she wasn't addressing him. His human-ing skills weren't the greatest on his best days anymore, and with today being the kick-off of the Pineville Rodeo in Pineville, Oregon, he'd been up since the butt-crack of dawn without an additional hit of caffeine. And now at ten a.m., Mr. Friendly Pants he was not.

"Hello up there. Excuse me?"

She *was* talking to him. Damn.

He took a deep breath of high desert air and shifted in his saddle. His horse, Dutch, flicked his ears, but otherwise remained motionless beneath him. "Yeah?" he said without looking down at yet another eager rodeo buckle bunny. He was supposed to be keeping an eye on his stock before they made their way down the town's main drag, but the hypnotic up and down motion of Mary Jo's bottom as she and the other rodeo royalty circled their mounts in front of him was, well, hypnotic.

"Would you mind moving your horse off my foot?"

Horror jolted through him in the split second before he

brought his heels and hands up to send Dutch in a hop sideways away from the woman. He looked down, prepared to see his horse crushing some poor lady's instep. Bodie blinked and pushed his hat back at the sight of Dutch's parade-ready black hoof planted on the toe of a bright yellow shoe.

A three-foot-long, vibrant yellow shoe with fire engine-red laces. Clown shoes.

His hands tingled like he'd just reached the top fence rail as a bull's horn breezed his britches. While certain the female clown the shoe belonged to hadn't suffered any injury, he still nudged his horse over a step.

She smiled at him from under her red rubber nose. "Thanks. I hated to disrupt your enjoyment of Miss Udder Salve's departure…" She set her huge rainbow wig a-bobbing by nodding toward the group of sequin-laden riders trotting in a circle before it was their turn to head down little Pineville's Main Street.

Bodie snorted. "Dairy Queen. Newly crowned."

"Good for her." She sounded genuine despite her wisecrack. "I think I'm supposed to start down the parade route after the Butter Babes—"

He chuckled. Maybe not entirely genuine.

She frowned and looked behind her. "Though I don't see the guys…"

Bodie only saw what had to be the sexiest clown on earth. All those little boys who grew up afraid of clowns were approaching the concept all wrong. Just the thought of what she might *not* have on under her armpit-high, white and red striped pants had him edging Dutch back toward her just in case the opportunity to peek down the hooped opening of her pants should present itself. Not that he would peek, but just in case. He was a guy after all. His Romeo days might have been over, but he couldn't help basic biology.

Her white T-shirt was respectably—and annoyingly— loose and thick, probably to protect her shoulders from the wide black canvas suspenders holding her ridiculous britches up. But he sensed curves worth exploring.

Not by him, though.

Since the accident five years ago, despite his reputation, he hadn't really been tempted by any woman, let alone one sporting a red rubber nose and a rainbow afro. But there was something about the large, world-weary tear painted at the corner of her big blue right eye that tugged at something deep in his scarred belly. He wanted to pluck off the goofy nose and kiss her silly.

Which would be about as smart as getting on the back of a bull again.

When she didn't find who she was apparently looking for, she shrugged and returned her attention to him. Or, more accurately, the big gelding lazing beneath him. She gave his very unflappable horse a pat that turned to a scratch. Dutch shifted his weight toward her, and his muscular shoulder flexed, his hide twitching when she hit the sweet spot.

She *cooed* at the big idiot. "Yes, I didn't think I'd be going anywhere with such a strapping boy as you looking so comfortable standing on my shoe."

Dutch turned and nuzzled her good.

Now his dang horse probably knew what she had on under those pants. Bodie shifted in the saddle again, unnerved by his sudden fixation on clown undergarments. He turned his attention to where his bulls were milling about in the temporary pens set up in the parking lot of Pineville's lone supermarket at the end of Main Street.

Some bulls could be corralled together because the only fights they had to pick in this world were with the cowboys who climbed aboard their backs and tried to cling like tenacious ticks for eight long seconds. But others, such as Boomerang, wanted to fight everyone he made eye contact with. Man or beast. So Boomerang always had his own pen. And he was currently pawing a hole in the heat-softened asphalt to apparently make his break à la *The Great Escape.* He was a handful. Which was why he had his own mounted escort on parade day.

Bodie didn't like to take chances.

Not anymore. Especially now that he had finally regained a spot on the rodeo circuits. Not as the top-twenty-ranked bull rider he'd once been, but as a stock contractor in his own right with his own bulls.

Knowing he didn't want to have to pay for a pavement patch to Frank's Groceries' parking lot, Bodie caught the eye of Danny, Boomerang's wrangler for today, and with nothing more than a hitch of his chin, conveyed the need to redirect the bull's current fascination with digging an escape hole outta here.

As he watched Danny clamor over the metal pen rails,

Bodie heard a nearby group of teenagers complain, "Where are the bulls? These are just a bunch of cows."

He stifled a sigh and scratched at his short beard. Maybe the kids had skipped anatomy class. Or didn't know that just because his bulls didn't have horns, they didn't buck any less. They were simply a little less deadly. Just a little.

"But I bet you can really move when you want to, can't you?" His new favorite clown said and brought his attention back to her.

She was stroking Dutch's shiny black cheek and the way her arm crossed over her chest, he couldn't help but notice her cleavage. Clowns weren't supposed to have cleavage. When she glanced up at him, he flinched at being caught checking out her chest. But she *did* have great cleavage.

"He has some Arabian in him, doesn't he?" she asked.

Bodie instantly focused on a cowboy's second favorite subject, his horse. He planted his forearm on his thigh so he could lean down toward her and found himself inadvertently diving headfirst into her clear-blue eyes. He stared for just a half a beat too long before he remembered he had some remanence of a brain and forced himself to focus on answering her question. "Yes, he does. You must really know your horseflesh. His dam is a blooded Arab. My dad only crossbred her because we had this Quarter Horse stud that was so barrel-chested he—"

"Whoa, whoa." She held up her hands and grinned. "I don't know *that* much about horses. I'm afraid I'm one of those annoying types who knows a little about a lot of things, but not enough to carry on more than a two-minute conversation."

"But knows enough to be dangerous?"

"Yep." Her grin all but disappeared beneath her rubber nose and was definitely at odds with the big tear meticulously painted at the corner of her eye.

He really wanted to know the story behind that tear.

And he had absolutely no intention of finding out.

Yet he found himself saying, "I bet I could find something to talk to you about for more than two minutes." *What the hell?* Was it those eyes? Or that tear? Nah, it was the cleavage. Just proved he wasn't dead.

Her tongue slipped out to moisten her unpainted lips. His gut reacted by clenching as if taking a punch.

"I bet you could." Her voice was sexy even with the rubber nose.

He was doomed.

"And here all this time I've been stuffing my feet into pumps and wiggling into dinky miniskirts, when all I needed to do was dress like a clown so I can land a contract with the rodeo circuit to catch a guy's attention. They should tell us these things in junior high."

Thoroughly distracted by the mention of pumps and dinky miniskirts, he was startled when Dutch began to fidget. It was their turn to head down the parade route.

Reluctantly, he turned toward Danny, who had been watching him with a smirk Bodie was going to have to introduce to some dirt at a later date, and gave him a wave to start the bulls down Main Street. They'd let Boomerang go first because the bull would cause less ruckus that way. And seeing as Boomerang tipped the scales at over eighteen hundred pounds of pure Brahman bull, horns or no, he was dang impressive trotting down a street. Not a bad advertisement for the Hadley Cattle Company.

Bodie let out a quick whistle that caught the attention of Cabe, who'd been chatting up one of the Butter Babes. A grin tugged at the corners of Bodie's mouth at the new moniker he wouldn't be able to shake. Cabe was clearly flirting with a member of the court as they both sat atop their horses facing in opposite directions. Very romantic, but not what either was supposed to be doing.

With just the slightest tip of his head toward the bulls, Bodie reminded Cabe what they were here for, and his youngest employee said his goodbyes to the lady and wheeled his bay toward the pens to start the rest of the bulls down the street.

Because Bodie was local—his family's ranch lay a mere ten miles away—and his bulls had been consistently high scoring in the other regional rodeos he'd contracted with, he'd been asked to supply eight bulls for this year's Pineville Rodeo. The most bulls he'd been contracted to supply since he'd jumped into the bucking bull game three years ago, two years after his career-ending wreck at one of the biggest national bull riding events. His family had been well established in the rodeo stock contracting business by his grandfather, but the bulls were all his. He sat taller in the saddle. Things were finally starting to go his way.

He returned his attention to the curbside of the street and the most stirring clown he'd ever encountered. She was once again scanning the crowd, but obviously not seeing whomever she was searching for. He held Dutch steady so he could reach down and coax a lock of what turned out to be long, honey-blond hair out from beneath her rainbow wig.

She blinked as if just waking and clapped a hand over her wig. "Hey, why'd you do that?"

With Dutch itching to be on the move along with the bulls and the guys, Bodie answered, "So I'll know you when I see you around the rodeo grounds."

And be able to avoid her like a sharp-spurred bull.

"And at the sponsors' meet 'n greet party tonight?"

Was that hope in her voice or simply an invitation?

Though his interest was piqued, he pushed away the attraction. Ever since Elizabeth Howe had dumped him after seeing how badly scarred he was and realizing he wouldn't be riding bulls anymore, he'd sworn off romance. Plus, he hadn't gone to any after-party since the accident. He wasn't a fan of pity.

Clown-girl had mentioned in a roundabout way that she wanted to get contracted with the rodeo circuit, so odds were not in his favor of being able to dodge her indefinitely. But he would cross that bridge when he came to it.

Without taking his eyes off her, he let Dutch start walking away. He tipped his hat to her. "Have fun at the sponsors' party."

She tried to put her hands on her hips, but the size of her clown pants kept her from making contact. "What makes you think I'm going?"

He wheeled Dutch around. "You'll be there," he challenged her. He took the chance she was the type who couldn't resist a challenge. She was, after all, wearing three-foot-long yellow clown shoes.

"We'll see," she hedged, her chin up. But she smiled the slightest of smiles, in raging contrast to her costume but in perfect harmony with the tear painted on her cheek.

For some stupid reason, Bodie felt like he had when he'd successfully bred his first bull.

He swung Dutch back toward his bulls when he heard her yell, "You could have just asked me my name."

Using the sudden need to readjust his tan cowboy hat as an excuse to ignore the laughter of Cabe and Danny and everyone else within earshot, he heaved a sigh at his own idiocy. But there was no getting around it. He was *rusty* and now everyone knew it. He turned in the saddle. "What *is* your name?" he yelled back.

She hesitated, the rainbow afro bobbing on her head as she looked down at her huge shoes.

He was about to ride back toward her when the wig bobbed upward.

"Cait."

"Kate," he repeated and tipped his hat again in acknowledgment. Right back in self-satisfied mode, he faced forward again, confident he would have no trouble at all avoiding the honey-haired, gorgeous, blue-eyed Kate after the official kick-off of the Pineville Rodeo.

"CAITLIN ANN NEISSON, are you insane?" Amanda Rodrigues, Caitlin's best friend for most of her twenty-five years and the one person in the whole world more stubborn than herself, practically hissed in Caitlin's ear. She batted at Caitlin's rainbow clown wig when the polyester strands stuck to her Rodeo Royalty Court-issued high-shine lip gloss.

"What are you talking about?" Caitlin flattened her wig on the offending side and turned to her friend.

"Him." She pointed.

Caitlin followed the line of Amanda's finger and met the glaring gaze of a bearded middle-aged man. "Maybe he doesn't like clowns."

Amanda scoffed. "Not him. That cowboy."

Caitlin had a sneaking suspicion who Amanda was referring to. With a kernel of a plan sprouting in her brain to secure the help she needed, Caitlin had still been staring at his broad, muscular back and, well, other things, when Amanda had run—literally run—Rumbles toward her. Amanda had leapt off next to Caitlin, fringes flying and her sparkles sparkling, while Rumbles was still skidding to a stop.

"The one in the black, logo-covered shirt and tan hat?"

"On the big black gelding. Yes, Caitlin. Do you have any idea who that is?" She arched a parade-perfect brunette brow at Caitlin. Amanda really did deserve to be on the court. Caitlin would have to remember to tell her as much.

"No, I don't know who he is. He didn't tell me his name. We talked about his horse, and—"

"You are kidding me! Do you know what your brothers would do if they saw you talking to him? They would never let you leave the ranch ever, ever again. And we both know how much you'd like that." Their eyes locked, blue and chocolate brown, a vivid memory of a summer gone wrong replaying in both their minds.

They had been fifteen. An idyllic summer of sleepovers and campouts. And then everything changed one late August afternoon when Caitlin, left to her own devices because Amanda had been needed at her family's ranch, had been in the bull barn giving treats to the bulls when she heard her mother's raised voice inside the vault. She'd barely crossed the threshold into what was normally her grandfather's domain when her mom spotted her and hurried her back out. As her mom hustled her out through the bull barn's paddock, saying they needed to find her grandfather, her grandfather's prize bull made an unexpected appearance in the paddock. Right on the heels of Caitlin and her mother. Her mom suffered the brunt of the animal's uncharacteristic fury, but miraculously survived. Barely.

In a fury of his own, her grandfather put the bull down, despite its value, as well as destroyed the straws containing its future progeny. Her mom spent the next ten years a bedridden prisoner of a broken body and mind in a near constant fight for her life. Caitlin became a prisoner of a different sort, terrified of the bulls she'd once loved and smothered by family members horrified by the accident in the paddock.

Amanda's shudder broke the spell. "And your cousins! They will kill you! Then *slaughter* him."

The men of her family going after any man who might be interested in her...reason number twenty-four why she'd left the ranch for good as soon as she could. Or so she'd thought. After completing her undergrad and graduate degree in Fine Arts at the state university, attending year around, she had planned to never have to be around bulls ever again by finding a teaching job in Portland or Seattle. But wasn't there a saying about best laid plans? When her mother had taken a turn for the worse almost six months ago, Caitlin had given up her job search and returned home to be present when her mother finally succumbed to the injuries she'd suffered just over a decade ago. So here Caitlin was, back where she'd never thought she'd be, and facing what seemed to be an impossible task.

Caitlin held up her hands. "Okay, okay, Amanda, I get the picture. The boys don't like the guy. Why? Who is he? Whose girl did he poach?" She looked back toward the pens where her mystery cowboy had headed. A man as gorgeous as that? Had to be a woman involved somehow.

She thought of his square chin and straight nose, then something struck her. "Is he a Hadley? He looks like a Hadley." Her grandfather had been competing with the Hadleys for the lion's share of the rodeo stock contract for years, and never had a kind word for them. A habit the rest of her family had picked up as a matter of course. Personally, Caitlin didn't get it.

"Yeah. Those are his people. But it's much, much worse than just that." Amanda put her hand gently on Caitlin's arm the way she used to right before she'd explain how terribly flawed Caitlin's plans for mayhem always were. Amanda squeezed her arm slightly as if making sure she had

Caitlin's full attention.

She did.

"Caitlin, listen to me. He's Bodie Hadley. *The* Bodie Hadley. The guy who insisted on riding Porky Chop, even after everyone warned him not to. He is the bull rider responsible for your cousin's death by grandstanding instead of hightailing it out of the ring after the buzzer, like he was supposed to."

Caitlin blanched, her mind swirling around the idea that had begun to form at the sight of all those hornless, seemingly congenial bulls. Maybe he wasn't the perfect man for the job of providing her with the help she needed. But did she have a choice?

CHAPTER TWO

"YOUR FRIENDS ARE sitting at the table right behind you, FYI."

Caitlin jumped in her seat, bumping her knee on the banquet table when her oldest brother, Ian, spoke directly in her ear. The dangling strings of lights in the tent of the sponsors' party cast shadows on his face. She hadn't noticed Ian sit back down next to her. She'd been working hard to ignore her next oldest brother, Liam's, ridiculous *I do have a very particular set of skills* routine delivered in between huge bites of cake. He rolled the impression out every time their two younger brothers dared him with a chaser of varying amounts of tequila. They were enough to make her crazy.

She darted a quick look at their father seated on her right. Dad was staring down at his paper plate, absently using his plastic fork to push around the beef ribs, potato salad, and baked beans she'd dished up for him. As far as she could tell, he hadn't eaten a bite. Her heart pulsed with an all too familiar ache. Mom had been gone almost six months now. A blink of the eye and an eternity all in one. But at least Mom was no longer in pain.

"Assuming," Ian's deep voice caught her attention again,

and she met his disturbingly knowing deep blue gaze, "your friends were who you've been craning your neck trying to spot the entire time we've been here."

They weren't. She'd already talked to most of them after the parade to learn more about a certain cowboy. The general consensus was Bodie had been the quintessential Rodeo Romeo as well as a top-twenty ranked bull rider before his awful wreck.

"Oh, what a coincidence." She made a show of glancing over her shoulder in surprise, even though she'd seen—not to mention heard—the table full of rodeo pageant court members. Thankfully, the girls had understood her tonight's-not-a-good-night-to-engage-the-Neisson-clan subtle head-shake when she'd first arrived. The girls were now fully occupied with the evening's latest gossip.

She sent Ian a wide smile. "How's that for handy."

Ian grunted and speared a bite of chocolate sheet cake. He was far too perceptive for her liking. Even as a kid, Ian usually knew when she was up to something. Usually. And he never hesitated to rat her out. All the boys in her family considered keeping an eye on her to be some kind of sacred duty. But Ian took his protectiveness to whole other level.

Especially now with Mom and Grandma gone.

She hated the smothering, the hovering, the protective-ness. She understood the whys of their behavior. If their mother hadn't veered away from Caitlin in the paddock at the last second, with a shout to draw the bull's attention, Caitlin would have been trampled too. She understood they intended to do everything in their power to keep her safe, but she hated it nonetheless.

In an effort to distract herself as well as her oldest brother, she asked, "Do you want some cake? I can get you some cake."

Ian froze with a fork-full of cake halfway to his mouth. *Oops.*

He raised his blond brows, a shade lighter than hers from endless hours spent on horseback tending his valuable herds of rodeo bucking broncs, roping steers and a select few rank bulls. Slowly he set his fork and bite of cake back down on the plate next to his half-eaten slice. Leaning back in his chair until it squeaked, he considered her again.

She inwardly cringed, hooking her booted feet around the legs of her folding chair. If she told him she was looking for a cowboy, and *which* cowboy, he'd lock her in the nastiest stall he could find for sure.

He cocked his head to the side, the way he always did when he was taking the true measure of a member of the herd, and narrowed his eyes. "What'cha up to, peanut?"

She opted for telling him the truth. Sort of. "Okay. I *am* looking for someone I met today during the parade, when you guys dressed me up like a full-blown clown."

He snorted a laugh and tried to cover it up by wiping at his mouth with his white paper napkin from his lap.

"Which I discovered, thanks to Amanda's uncle, Old Red, they don't require of bullfighters anymore, and not even all the barrelmen—especially the shoes, for obvious reasons. You guys made me dress up like the clowniest of clowns, then you didn't even show up for the parade. I was out there all by myself in that hot, silly costume."

"Consider it an initiation." Ian shrugged.

"More like hazing," she groused.

"You met someone…" He clung to her statement in his usual way. Ian never let anything slide. If a job needed done, he'd finish it. If he owed you a favor, consider it done. If you tried sneaking out of your window after curfew, he'd be the one standing in the dark to scare the snot out of you, shoving you right back inside with nothing more than "Back to bed, peanut."

She sighed, and glanced again at their father, other brothers, and cousin to see if they were listening. Liam was no longer carrying on about his *particular set of skills* and had angled his head toward them more than before, but Caitlin couldn't tell if he was listening to her and Ian or not. Drew was destroying a huge barbequed turkey leg with his face. Alec was watching Drew with the sort of wonder and awe only the youngest brother could muster. Her oldest cousin Jack had his chin propped on his hand and was gazing wistfully at the table full of feminine rodeo royalty.

She frowned at Alec. He didn't appear the slightest bit worried about what he intended to do this week. Bravery? Or stupidity? He'd actually need a hearty dose of each, in her opinion. Both of them would.

She realized it really didn't matter if Liam, Drew, Alec, or Jack were listening. Ian would fill the other boys in regardless. He might not burden Dad. Then again, maybe he would. He definitely wouldn't tell Grandfather.

She turned back and met Ian's sharp gaze again. "Yes.

Someone who, I hope, will teach me what I'm beginning to suspect you all"—she hitched her chin at the other occupants of the round banquet table—"won't."

Her oldest brother's nostrils flared.

She was in for it, now.

"Come again?"

Knowing her best defense had always been a strong offense, she cut to the chase. "You're just humoring me, Ian. You guys will never let me—"

Her father's deep, care-worn voice broke into the conversation. "I said you could train to bullfight, Caitlin Ann. So train."

Caitlin swiveled in her chair to face her father seated on her other side, but he hadn't moved. Hadn't looked up from his plate. Had she imagined him speaking? "Dad?"

Liam pushed his crumb-scattered cake plate toward the center of the table and planted a heavy forearm in its place. "Why, Dad? Why should we let her risk her life in the arena with a bull when she hasn't even been on a horse since—"

Ian snapped, "Enough, Liam."

Dad finally raised his face to meet Liam's, then Caitlin's gaze. What she saw in his light blue eyes broke her heart a million times over.

Dad placed his rope-roughened hand over hers and gave a light squeeze. "Do what makes your heart happy, girl. If you think dodging bulls is going to make you happy, then dodge them." He patted her hand, then picked his fork up and went back to pushing his food around.

Realization hit her. Her father was the one placating her.

She could hear the mollifying in his tone, the almost dismissive way he told her to go ahead and do what she wanted. Her brothers and cousins might be giving her the runaround and hazing treatment, but they at least knew they had to keep her out of the arena.

Her father, on the other hand, didn't believe she actually intended to go through with becoming a rodeo protection athlete. He didn't think she had what it took to face a bull, *mano a mano*, so to speak, by distracting the bull to help a rider get clear after he was either bucked off or bailed willingly. Something her bullfighting cousins had been doing for years.

He didn't think she'd do it. He didn't think she'd go through with the rigors of the training or face the reality of the danger literally head-on.

She met the stormy blue gaze of her younger brother Alec, who'd clearly been listening after all, and waited for him to fess up to his part. She was having to do this because of him, after all.

He remained silent, and she wasn't surprised when his attention dropped to the vacant tabletop between them. She had to admit to herself that, ultimately, this had been her decision, but he didn't have to leave her twisting in their brothers' scrutiny.

Caitlin rose from her seat. "Alec, come help me get some more cake."

Alec's gaze leapt to hers, but he didn't move, so she rounded the table and gave a quick tug on the back of his shirt.

"Now," she insisted in the way reserved for older siblings.

He pushed away from the table and stood up, blessedly ignoring the fact that, aside from Liam, everyone still had various amounts of cake in front of them.

Sidestepping one of the top bull riders, Josh Caldwell, and the cluster of sponsors he was holding court with, Caitlin led Alec to the long table against the side of the tent where the caterer had laid out pre-sliced pieces of chocolate and white cake on small paper plates. She pretended to struggle with the choice between the two types of cake.

"What, Caitlin?"

Without looking at her little brother, Caitlin whispered, "You know exactly *what*, Alec. Why aren't you helping me?"

He turned to her. "Because you don't have to do this, Cait."

"Yes, I do." She shot him a look. "You know I do. After you told Mom you were going to ride bulls—"

"That's not what happened. It was like she knew she didn't have long left. A day before she...she passed, she was lucid enough to ask me what I would do if I could do anything in the world—"

"And you told her you would be a champion bull rider."

Alec straightened to his full, six-one height. At nineteen, he had his height, but he had yet to fill out. "I did. Because it's true. I couldn't lie to her. It's what I'd planned to do before she was run over by that damn bull."

"You were *nine* when that happened."

"Yeah. A nine-year-old who'd dreamed of riding his grandpa's bulls. But after what happened in the paddock..."

Alec shook his head as if he had no words to convey what essentially losing his mother had done to his nine-year-old self. "No way could I put Dad and everyone else through the stress of me riding bulls after that. But she made me promise I'd go for it, that I would give it an honest shot."

Caitlin leaned toward him to keep from being overheard and said, "Then she made me promise to do everything I could to keep you safe. The least you could do is back me up."

Alec reared back. "She didn't."

Caitlin heaved a sigh at her little brother's cluelessness. "She did, Alec. I would never make up something like that." She glanced at the table where their family was seated. Only Ian and Liam were watching them, the suspicion on their faces plain. She turned back to the dessert table and grabbed two plates of whatever cake was closest.

Alec followed her lead and managed to balance four plates in his hands. His expression pensive, he said, "Mom loved us, Cait. Maybe getting me to go after my dream and you to face your fears was the only way she could think of to show us."

Caitlin had nothing to say to her brother's logic, and simply stared after him as he took the cake plates back to their family. There was no way for her to know if he was right or not.

But she did know one thing. Their dad was wrong.

She did have what it takes.

And she would keep Alec safe like she'd promised their mom, even if she had to go hunt down the help she needed.

Caitlin followed Alec back to their table, depositing the cake-filled paper plates in the center of the table as Alec had. Drew and Jack immediately reached for one, even though they'd already had a piece.

As she retook her seat, her attention was snagged by three men entering the tent through the entrance to the left of the band.

Liam saw them, too, and grumbled, "Those damn Hadleys, showing up just in time to monopolize the rodeo officials."

A trick her grandfather had perfected over the years to secure rough stock contracts before his competition—namely the Hadleys—ever had a chance.

There had been bad blood between her family and the Hadleys for Caitlin's entire life, though she had no idea why. The competition wasn't simply for rodeo rough stock contracts. The boys had competed for spots on the rodeo team, for girls, for everything strapping young men vied for.

Her pulse quickening, Caitlin straightened in her chair to better see the new arrivals. While there was definitely a resemblance to Bodie Hadley in their dark hair, broad shoulders and attractive features, he wasn't with them. But to make sure, she asked, "Which ones are those?"

Liam practically growled, "Jacob, Garrett and Ben." He didn't seem inclined to specify who was who. The older of the three must be Bodie's father, with the other men being his brothers.

Definitely no Bodie. Caitlin slumped back against her chair. She'd been trying to watch all the entrances—there were four—on the chance Bodie showed up tonight. According to Amanda, he'd be breaking with his past behavior of avoiding official rodeo functions since he'd been gored and her cousin killed, but a girl could hope. Amanda had doubted he would show up. Caitlin had been crossing her fingers the entire night regardless.

But truth be told, she wasn't sure if she wanted him to come to the party tonight or not. Now that she'd decided she would ask him for help, she was nervous about seeing him again. Especially when she hadn't been able to stop thinking about how attractive she found him, and the fact that, as far as her family was concerned, he was the enemy for simply being a Hadley.

IT WAS NEARLY midnight and Bodie had been doing a hell of a good job of avoiding Kate. With every check of his bulls, someone sought him out to update him on the whereabouts of a strawberry-blond Kat, a dark blond Kim, and the undaunted Mary Jo that had offered to lighten her brown mane after word had spread he was looking for a blonde, even though he adamantly denied looking for anyone. There had been a lot of witnesses to his ham-fisted flirting this afternoon, and now he was paying the price.

The only reason he hadn't put a fast and decisive end to the nonsense was because Old Red Rodrigues, a member of the local rodeo circuit old guard, had wandered over to the pens and made an off-hand comment about how surprised—

and pleased—he was to hear Bodie had been talking to cute-as-a-bug-Caitlin before the parade today.

A warning horn louder than a thousand completed ride buzzers had gone off in Bodie's head when he'd heard the name, but he couldn't put his finger on why. And now he needed to figure out the answer. So here he was, still up, walking amongst the trailers behind the rodeo grounds, when he should be in bed.

Even though he told himself nothing would come of this night, he wound his way through the trailer town that sprouted up at each venue, counting on the cold high desert air to clear his head.

Who the hell was this Kate? Or was she Caitlin? And why did he have to know? Was he starting to slip toward his dangerous compulsions of acting without thinking and catering to his baser needs again? Or was he just a fool?

At the last row of trailers, campers, and motor homes, he started to wonder if he'd imagined the primitive connection he'd felt surge between him and the woman he only knew as Kate when he'd looked into those big blue eyes of hers. Or was Red right and Bodie had mistaken her name?

If he hadn't imagined what he'd felt and couldn't shake the connection, he knew he shouldn't be out here right now. Definitely dangerous.

So he turned to head back to his own rig. The rodeo grounds were close enough to his family's property that he could just go back to the ranch and his own bed, but he'd decided to bring the fifth wheel out and set up near the bull pens so he could keep an eye on Boomerang himself. That bull was mischief on cloven hooves.

Something stopped him in his tracks. It wasn't a sound so much as a rippling in the air, a shift in the temperature toward hot. He pivoted and saw a woman emerge from between the trailers and walk away from him. She wasn't walking like most of the women he knew, though, with unyielding denim and overly optimistic size choices.

This woman's jeans fit her more like a well-worn glove than a girdle, and her gait was more like an athlete than a seductress, her cadence smooth and lithe. And, to him, one of ancient sexuality. It wasn't just the straight, dark blond hair hanging down her back that made him certain she was his Kate. He refused to get metaphysical enough to wonder at how he knew, considering her last getup.

He just knew.

"Hey!" he called out, then winced at how loud, not to mention uncouth, he sounded. What the *hell* was he thinking?

She stopped with a start and looked over her shoulder at him, seeming to relax when clearly recognized him.

"Kate, nice night." He tried again as he walked toward her, sounding so much more suave he thought with a mental snort.

"That it is." She didn't sound impressed with his choice of opener, but she did sound sexy without the rubber nose. She pointed at the spot where she'd emerged from between the trailers. "Were you following me?"

"No. I only just now saw you." He had been looking for her, sort of, but he hadn't been following her.

"Huh." She looked toward the spot she'd come from. "I could have sworn someone was following me."

"Wasn't me." When he reached her, he was struck not only by her looks—thank God he hadn't merely developed the hots for clowns—but also her height. Dutch was a big horse so he hadn't noticed how tall she was while he was in the saddle and she was on the ground. The unwanted image of all the places they would nicely fit together popped into his mind.

He had to clear his throat before he could talk again.

"I'm sorry." He snatched his hat from his head. "I haven't properly introduced myself. The name's Bodie Hadley. At your service, ma'am." Okay, he was laying it on thick, but he couldn't seem to help himself.

"You *are* Bodie Hadley."

"In the flesh." Such as it was, he thought sourly.

She gave him that little smile again, her mouth truly luscious without a clown nose overshadowing it. "You said you would be at the party tonight."

"Did I?" He hadn't gone near the party. No way, no how. Too many curious and pitying folks to contend with. "I sent Cabe. That kid is charm wrapped in denim."

She nodded, not looking at all surprised. "Because you never go to those parties anymore."

Someone had been giving her a crash course in Bodie Hadley.

A very unpleasant sensation started fluttering in the pit of his stomach. Early on, after his wreck, in the wake of Elizabeth breaking up with him, he'd encountered one too many buckle bunnies wanting to get a peek at the damage done to him by Porky Chops and then not being able to handle the reality. He'd decided to pass on repeating that experience some time ago.

"I always assumed everything I've heard about you was exaggerated."

The very unpleasant sensation stopped fluttering and started stomping and kicking at his guts.

"I mean, they said you were good-looking, but you're really…" she trailed off, waving a hand at him like he was something she couldn't quite comprehend.

The storm going off in his innards relented that she hadn't been referring to his scars. He grinned, inanely flattered that such a pretty woman found him attractive. "Really? What? A snappy dresser?" He straightened the collar of the crisp white shirt he'd changed into earlier, then tugged suggestively on his championship belt buckle. "A sparkling conversationalist? Speaking of which, we have a bet to settle."

"What?"

His gaze inadvertently dropped to where her breasts were hinted at beneath her chambray shirt. His fingers started to itch to find out exactly what she was hiding.

What was wrong with him? Why now? Why this woman?

The tiny hairs at the nape of his neck stood on end, and he firmly ignored them.

He met her remarkable gaze, the blue smoky in the near darkness. Kate was definitely one he would have to warn off. He wouldn't be able to bear the look of revulsion in her beautiful eyes. Better she think him a bastard than pity him.

He best cowboy up. "Now, about that bet…"

"Bet?"

He cocked a knee and slanted one hip toward her, his body humming to touch hers, but he ignored it the way he ignored most of his discomforts. Most. "Yes. I bet you I could find something to talk to you about for more than two minutes, remember?"

"Yeah, but—"

"What super power would you rather have?"

"Excuse me?" Her finely arched brows came together sharply, her confusion clear.

He returned his hat to his head and pulled his phone from his back pocket and checked the time. "I'm starting my two minutes now. What super power would you want?"

"Ah. Okay, we're doing this now…" She straightened up and gripped her hands in front of her, worrying her fingers. She took a deep breath and said, "Um…time travel."

Interesting. "I'm not sure if that's a super power, but…I guess if you want to be Orson Welles Woman—" He shrugged as he struggled to suppress his grin.

She slumped against the trailer. "What would you pick?"

"Super strength, of course. Show those bulls who's boss." He tried to keep his tone light, but she already knew who he was, so he probably sounded lame.

"Speed is better than strength. It's always better."

He inched closer to her, closing the space between them. "Not always," he said on an exhale, bringing his mouth closer to hers.

She lifted her face toward his, her gaze fastened on his mouth. She caught her lower lip between her teeth. Heat surged through him so hard and fast he was surprised his hat didn't fly off his head.

She released her lip, looked him in the eye, and said, "Definitely. Sometimes slow is definitely better."

"Mmhmm," he agreed as she brought her full mouth within a centimeter of his, their breath blended in a hot melody.

Of course, he had been kicked in the head in recent years.

He knew she'd be infinitely kissable, and Bodie's pulse went from pounding to roaring. She smelled sweet, like she'd been drinking cola, and he wouldn't be able get enough of her.

Another warning bell went off in his head. Nothing could come of this. There was no point in doing this to either one of them. It was cruel to even start anything physical when he knew how the encounter would end. How his few previous amorous attempts had ended since that fateful day.

The flash of horror on his date's face before it was replaced by something more kind, more socially acceptable like…

Pity.

He'd had more than enough pity.

He'd rather be known as an asshole than be pitied.

He started to pull away from the almost kiss when she wrapped her arms around his neck, brought her lush body tight against his, and kissed him hard. Bodie grabbed hold of her hips and did his best to extract her, fighting the sensations she was stirring as best he could.

And losing.

Because he'd lose his mind if she kept kissing him like she was, meeting the strokes and thrusts of his tongue with hers, like certain other parts of them would meet if he could go all the way with her.

But he wouldn't.

He couldn't.

He could have this moment with her, though, until he forced her to classify him as just another jerk in this world.

It was time to go.

Bodie pulled his mouth from hers and put some distance between them. "You've convinced me, Kate," he rasped, fighting to catch his breath and maintain his control.

She went up on her toes to nibble on his ear, knocking his hat askew. "My name is actually Caitlin."

"Oh, geez, sorry. So you *are* Red's 'cute-as-a-bug-Caitlin.'"

"Mmhmm," she murmured, kissing her way toward his mouth. He arched his neck away from her sweet torture. If she reached his mouth again, he'd be doomed.

"Well, Caitlin, it's been real, but I just remembered I have an equally hot babe waiting for me in my trailer." He peeled her arms from around his neck. "And technically, she has first dibs. Sorry, but I gotta go."

She grabbed ahold of his belt buckle and pressed her breasts into his chest. While the light from the currently occupied trailers and campers didn't quite reach them, he swore there was an odd, almost desperate glint in her beautiful eyes.

"Come on, cowboy. I have a proposition for you. My Airstream is just a row over. What do you say?"

CAITLIN COULDN'T BELIEVE she'd actually had the nerve to say the words. But she needed more time with him to ask for his help. All the girls had gone on and on about what a hound dog he'd been, and how he'd agree to anything if he thought he'd get some action in return.

She could promise him all sorts of things. No one said she had to pay up.

Though that kiss…best not to add hot, intense and oh, so delectable into the equation. She needed this man's help. And she'd rope him in one way or another.

He gently extracted himself from her. "Don't get me wrong, I'm really flattered, but—"

She cut him off before he could send her on her way. "Please. Can we go somewhere and just talk?" Realizing Ian or one of her other family members could have been the one she'd sensed following her and would be waiting for her in their trailer, she said, "Look, forget about my trailer. But can we go somewhere and talk? Just for a few minutes?"

Bodie heaved a sigh. "All right. Come on," he relented and gestured for her to follow him.

Shoring up her resolve, she fell into step with him. She

didn't believe for one second her brothers would do as their father said and let her train like an actual bullfighter. Liam would find a way to keep her out of the arena or, at the very least, force her to remain squatting down inside the barrel-man's barrel in the center of the rodeo ring. Relegated to the role of comic relief for the crowd and nothing more.

No, she needed to find someone outside of the Neisson family to help her.

She had no choice but to ask for help from one of the infamous Rodeo Romeos.

CHAPTER THREE

C AITLIN STOOD JUST inside the doorway of Bodie Hadley's fifth wheel trailer and gently pulled the door closed behind her. She timed her loud gulp of trepidation with the click of the door latch hitting home. She couldn't let him see how nervous she was being here, asking this of him.

Bodie, who'd preceded her into the trailer, paused in the act of lifting his tan cowboy hat off his head and glanced over his shoulder at her. "You're welcome to come on in. If you want, of course."

"Yes. Yes, absolutely." Caitlin moved away from the door. She quickly slipped behind Bodie as he returned his focus to hanging his hat on a peg mounted on the faux-wood paneled wall. She slid onto the U-shaped bench seat behind the trailer's white and gray speckled Formica table, shoving a partially coiled flank strap into a corner of the bench. Bodie must have been rebraiding the end of the soft cotton rope used to encourage a bull's bucking. Other than the wayward flank strap, a couple of halters, and a saddle set atop the couch at the back of the RV, the fifth wheel trailer was clean—surprisingly so for where they were. Granted, it still smelled of livestock and man. A smell from her childhood. While many of the RV rigs people used to travel the rodeo circuit were nicer than some peoples' homes because they spent as much or more time in them, Bodie's was definitely on the utilitarian side of decorating and amenities.

There were three mismatched coffee mugs turned upside down on a folded tea towel next to the sink. Probably used by Bodie and his crew. Or…she couldn't keep her gaze from straying to the closed pocket door up two steps at the front of the trailer.

"Don't worry," Bodie said as he moved to lean his backside against the sink counter opposite her. "We're alone."

"No hot babe with first dibs?" She hadn't really bought his claim of being already spoken for tonight, but she wanted to hear it from him.

Bodie snorted and crossed his arms over his chest. "No hot babe. Besides you, that is."

Her attention was inadvertently drawn to his thick biceps and muscled shoulders stretching the fabric of his crisp white buttoned-down shirt. Her cheeks grew warm and she realized she was flushing. What was wrong with her? She had four very fit brothers. She saw well-developed biceps every day. A small voice in the back of her brain whispered, *yeah, but this guy is* not *your brother.*

She jerked her gaze back up to his. "Why lie, then?"

He crossed one booted foot over the other and shrugged the way gorgeous men did when the subject of the presence—or lack of—a woman came up. "Easier than trying to explain the truth."

She raised a brow at him. "The truth being the fact that I'm a Neisson?"

His arms dropped away from his chest. "What?" Then comprehension dawned on his face. "You're Caitlin *Neisson*." He ran both hands over his face then recrossed his arms. "Yeah, you being a Neisson is definitely a great reason to claim I'm otherwise engaged." His gaze shifted to the closed pocket door then back to hers. "And begs the question, why, exactly, are you talking to me, among other things? Obviously, you know more about me than just my name."

Recalling the lecture, and stringent warning, she'd received this morning, Caitlin slowly nodded. "My friend, Amanda, told me."

"One of the Butter Babes?" His full mouth twitched at the edges, and the sparkle she'd seen in his eyes this morning when he'd seen her in her clown costume returned.

She grinned outright. He'd been paying attention. "Yes, Amanda is a Butter Babe."

"And she told you…what? To stay away from me?"

Caitlin slumped back against the fake leather-covered bench. She resisted the urge to wipe her increasingly sweaty palms against the seat—they would just slide—or her jeans-clad thighs. "Among other things," she echoed his words, but with a completely different meaning.

There was no point equivocating. Bodie had to already be well aware of exactly why her family hated him. Had anyone else been involved in Charlie's death, she felt certain her family would have understood it had been an accident. But because a Hadley had been involved, they'd taken the blame game to the next level.

Charlie had been more like a brother than a cousin, but as far as Caitlin was concerned, he'd been doing his job when he'd been killed five years ago. A very, very dangerous job.

One she had to master, and fast.

This time, she didn't resist the urge to wipe off the dampness from her palms on her jeans.

His boot leather squeaked when he uncrossed his ankles and his hips shifted against the counter edge. "So, again, why are you here?"

"I need your help."

He uncrossed his arms again and rested the heels of his hands on the edge of the counter on either side of him. "With what?" His suspicion was palpable.

"My youngest brother, Alec, wants to be a bull rider."

He shrugged again, this time without the Hot Guy attitude. "So? You all live on a bucking bull breeding farm. He can sub-in for the dummies on the younger bulls."

She shook her head. "He needs a mentor. Someone to show him what to do. On bulls that won't try to kill him. I can't let him get hurt."

"Then teach him golf. Or better yet, encourage him to become a pro bass fisherman. I hear there's big money in pro bass fishing. Don't you all have your own lake?"

It was her turn to scoff. "It's more of a pond. And it's part of the irrigation system." Exasperation mounting, she waved off the notion of Alec doing anything other than what he'd set his mind to. "Would you have listened to anyone telling you not to climb on the back of a bull when you were his age?"

"How old is he?"

"He's nineteen."

Bodie looked at his boot-tips and readjusted his backside against the counter. "No, I would not have. But I'd also been competing professionally from the day I turned eighteen, as well as having ridden as a junior as soon as they'd let me."

She sat forward. "Which is why I know you can help. You have as much, or more, experience then just about anyone around here."

"I don't know where you've been—frankly, I don't know much about you personally at all—but I'm pretty sure you're aware of how my career ended. The only experience I have that exceeds anyone around here is with how to screw up as spectacularly as possible in the arena and still be breathing."

He held her gaze with his, the gray of his eyes as hard as tempered steel, and she could tell he, too, was thinking of the person also involved in his screw up but *not* still breathing.

Caitlin looked away first. Despite the passage of time, the pain of losing Charlie was always there. A bone-deep bruise that would never heal. Along with the loss of her mother, her family had been through so much already. She couldn't allow any more.

Her determination surged, and she met his gaze again. "You have brothers, right?"

"Yes," he answered tightly.

"Would they listen to you?"

A muscle jumped in his jaw.

She pulled in a breath. "Exactly."

His gaze tracked the rise of her breasts and she was instantly distracted by the memory of their kiss. Her cheeks flamed with what had to be the heat of embarrassment. Why had she thought she could take that tack with him? She would never be rid of the taste of him, the heat radiating off him.

He pulled in a chest-expanding breath and shook his head. "No, not *exactly*. You know damn well why my brothers won't listen to me."

She could easily hazard a guess as to why Bodie's own family might question his judgement after his showboating led to his injury and Charlie's death, but admitting as much wouldn't help her plead her case. So instead she said, "I don't know a thing about your family."

He eyed her for a moment, then heaved a sigh. "I don't suppose you would. You're the proverbial princess in the tower, aren't you? Kept safe from the scruff of the world, right?"

"More like locked away," she muttered.

"What?"

"Nothing."

As if the mention of scruff made him itch, he raised a hand to scratch at his short, dark beard. "I guess it's understandable the old man wouldn't sully your pretty ears with talk of the Hadleys."

She tucked her chin. "My dad doesn't—"

"Not your dad. Your grandpa." He pointed in what she supposed was the direction of her family's ranch. "Old Man

Wright."

She dropped her gaze to the speckled table top. Bodie had hit the proverbial nail on the head. Her grandfather had literally banned the name Hadley from being spoken in their home. Even before Charlie's death. She met Bodie's turbulent gaze again and opened her mouth to ask him if he knew why, but he spoke first.

"Which brings me back to my original question. Why are you here, asking me, of all people, to help your brother? Last I looked, he was a grown-ass man."

"Barely nineteen."

"Like I said, a grown-ass man."

Frustration pounded at Caitlin's temples. Nothing tonight had gone the way she'd hoped. She'd have to find another solution. She blew out a noisy breath. "Fine, fine. Forget I asked. I just thought that, after everything you've been through, you'd be the perfect person—"

He leaned forward. "What do you know about what I've been through? You have no clue, lady."

She pressed her spine deeper into the padded seat, assaulted by memories of the sights, sounds, and even the smells of that day in the paddock with her mother.

The anger and self-pity bled from his face. Contrition and sympathy softened the flint of his eyes. "Crap, Caitlin. I'm sorry." He heaved another sigh and slid onto the bench seat next to her, scrunching up the bull-decorated rope between them. "I totally forgot about what happened to you and your mom." He reached a conciliatory hand toward her.

She dodged his sympathy by shifting her gaze to his tan

cowboy hat hanging on the wall. "It's fine. I'm fine. Don't worry about it."

But it wasn't fine. And she would never be fine again. She would forever be the girl who was right next to her mother when Blackjack, her grandfather's prized bull, had mowed her mother down. That's all she'd ever be unless she did this. She had to keep her promise, not just for her brother, but for herself.

She met Bodie's stone-gray gaze head-on. "Please. You have to help us."

"Us?"

With nothing to hook her feet around, she gripped the edge of the Formica table. "Me and my brother."

Bodie flattened the hand he'd offered but she'd ignored on the table top. "I get what you want me to do for your brother." He tipped toward her until he was in her space. "But how am I supposed to help you?"

Caitlin shifted on the padded bench until the faux leather squawked. What had she been thinking, seeking him, as he'd said, of all people, for help? There had to be someone else at the rodeo this year with the kind of experience, good and bad, that Bodie possessed.

The answer came to her in a flash.

"You know what?" She reached out and clasped the hand he still had splayed on the table. A jolt of awareness zinged through her the instant her skin touched his, amplifying when he curled his callus-roughened fingers around hers. She automatically tried to pull her hand back, but he held her trapped in his strong, warm grip. She cleared her throat. "I—

I'm fine. I don't need your help. I just thought of someone else who will teach Alec to bull ride and me to bullfight."

His grip on her fingers tightened to the brink of painful. "*What?*" The question sounded as if it had been pulled up through him from the heels of his cowboy boots.

"I said I just thought of someone else—"

"Did you say *teach you to bullfight?*"

Her boot heels clunked against the baseboard beneath the bench seat. "Yes. If Alec is going to climb on the back of a bull, I intend to be in the arena to help keep him safe."

Bodie released her hand and grew as still and stiff as a fence post. When he finally spoke, his voice sounded pulled from the red-cinder earth beneath them. "Over my dead body."

BODIE WAS SUDDENLY drowning in pain and horror, unwillingly transported back to the moment everything in his life changed from light to dark. With the fine, deep dirt of the rodeo arena filling his nose and mouth as he curled into the horn-shaped hole in his gut, he'd had a perfect view of Porky Chops drawing a bead on the bullfighter who was trying to distract the agitated bull away from Bodie.

Charlie Neisson hadn't stood a chance.

The sound of the bull's hooves coming down with the force of a dropped pickup truck onto the bullfighter's chest reverberated in Bodie's head. A sound that woke him from the familiar sweat-soaked nightmare whenever he tried to sleep without first working himself to exhaustion. And it had all been Bodie's fault.

He'd been told he didn't have the skill to ride a bone-deep mean bull like Porky Chops, but Bodie had been determined to prove them wrong. And he had. He'd stuck for the whole eight seconds. And his euphoria had been so consuming his only thought had been to celebrate, to draw the crowd into his high with whoops of joy instead of hauling ass to the fence and out of harm's way. He'd been told later that it was his shouts that had caught Porky Chops attention and diverted him from leaving the arena through the exit chute.

Bodie filled his lungs with a slow, deep breath and forced himself to refocus on the here and now. On the beautiful blond, blue-eyed woman he'd been on the verge of devouring not fifteen minutes ago.

He watched Caitlin blink at him, her luscious mouth dropping open slightly, as she clearly worked to process his response.

Then she frowned fiercely at him. "Excuse me?"

Obviously, Her Ladyship wasn't used to being told she couldn't have what she wanted. "Look, princess—"

She stopped him with a raised hand. "First of all, don't call me that." Irritation dripped from her voice.

He put his own hands up in surrender, but now that he'd pictured her as a princess in a tower, he seriously doubted he'd be able to shake the image, any more than he could forget her calling her friends Butter Babes.

She jabbed a finger at him. "Secondly, it's not up to you

what I do or don't do. I get enough of that at home, thank you very much."

Bodie *hmphed*. "Maybe the Neisson men are smarter than they look."

"No, they're not. I mean, they are, but not when it comes to—oh, never mind." Her exasperation was tangible. She started scooting away from him along the bench, her intent to leave plain.

Bodie said nothing. Her making a quick departure was the best thing for both of them.

She was halted mid-scoot by a loud, metallic banging of a sturdy set of knuckles rapping sharply on the door to his trailer. Caitlin raised her gaze to his. The fear in her eyes of being caught here, with him, cut through him like a knife. Why he cared was beyond him.

The banging stopped. Then a deep, male voice said, "Hadley? I know you're in there. Open up."

Whoever it was had a chest-rattling baritone that easily penetrated the metal trailer door. Judging by the look of expanding horror on Caitlin's face, the man standing outside was a relative of hers. She confirmed his suspicion by diving under the table.

Bodie tipped to the side so he could see her crouched and hiding beneath the table in the nook created by the bench.

Caitlin met his raised brows with a combination of furious *shushing* and waving him away. She was downright adorable huddled against the round metal table support. And she definitely didn't appreciate him grinning at her.

The banging resumed. "Bodie Hadley!" *Bang, bang.*

"It's Ian," Caitlin mouthed at him. At least that's what he thought she was trying to tell him.

Definitely not in the mood for more Neisson family drama, Bodie sat up and shoved himself from the bench seat. The banging on his door intensified. Ian, or whoever it was doing the knocking, seemed to have switched from knuckles to the side of his fist.

"Hold your horses," Bodie growled, but then he was struck by the thought that maybe the oldest of the Neisson brothers had seen Bodie kissing Caitlin earlier. Prince Charming he was not.

Bodie took a beat to steel himself before pushing open the trailer door.

It was indeed Ian Neisson banging away on his door. With sun-bleached blond hair sticking out from where he'd shoved his dark-brown cowboy hat back on his head, probably in agitation, Ian was an inch or two taller than Bodie. The height of the trailer only gave Bodie a slight sense of dominance. Ian Neisson was a big dude. His creased dark-wash jeans and light-colored button-down shirt were crispy clean. Ian must have been at the sponsors' party with his sister before she'd slipped away.

Ian had stepped back to avoid the outward swing of the trailer's door, but he moved forward again, putting one foot on the first of the trailer's fold-out steps as if he expected to be invited inside. Bodie planted his shoulder firmly against the doorframe and settled his weight on it to disabuse Ian of the notion he'd be coming in.

"Neisson."

Ian readjusted his hat on his head, clearly not used to being blocked from anywhere. The spats between the oldest brother and only sister must be popcorn-worthy entertainment.

"Hadley."

"To what do I owe the pleasure?"

"I need to talk to you." Ian gestured to the trailer, obviously wanting to come in and sit down. "Can we go inside?"

A part of Bodie wanted to invite Ian in to find his sister and watch the hooves and spit fly. The same part of him that had been hot to ride Porky Chop. He was trying to make a habit of ignoring that part of himself.

He readjusted his shoulder against the door frame and crossed his arms over his chest. "I'm fine right here. Go ahead and talk."

Ian heaved a sigh and planted his hands on his hips. "Have you seen my sister?"

The image popped into Bodie's head of a very delectable woman making like an armadillo under his trailer table at that exact moment. It was all he could do not to smirk. But he needed to find out if Caitlin's oldest watchdog of a sibling had seen Bodie doing his damnedest to become one with her. "Why would you think I've seen your sister?"

"She has some crazy notions in her head right now—"

"And coming to see me would be a crazy notion." Bodie nodded.

"In a word, yes."

"You're not wrong." Nor was Ian wrong about Caitlin's

plan to go into the arena as a bullfighter. Bodie straightened away from the doorframe. After what her family had been through—hell, both their families—her asking for his help was nothing short of insane.

Ian's shoulders slumped and he ran a hand down his face. "Anyway, if you do happen to see her—"

"It's not like I make a habit of hanging around the Neisson family trailer."

Ian straightened and if he'd had a ruff, it would have raised. "As well you shouldn't."

Bodie uncrossed his arms and raised his hands in surrender. "I'm not stupid."

"Really?" Everything about the other man went hard, and bore an uncanny resemblance to Old Man Wright, his maternal grandfather.

Some things never changed. Bodie did his best to shrug off the insult, but he was only human. He reached for the trailer door. "Goodnight, Neisson."

Ian lifted a staying hand. "Look, Bodie, I'm serious. If Caitlin knocks on your door, send her on her way. Please." The last word looked like it had tasted like cow shit in Ian's mouth.

As much as Bodie wanted to tell Ian to go to hell, he needed the man gone more. "Don't worry about me, Neisson. I know what I need to do."

Bodie gave Ian enough time to tug on the brim of his hat before swinging the trailer door shut in his face.

Shaking his head, Bodie turned and found the reason for Ian Neisson's unprecedented visit still on her hands and knees peering around the slide out's half wall. She rocked back, as if preparing to scuttle beneath the table again if Bodie hadn't been alone.

She whispered, "Is Ian gone?"

"Yes. Feel free to regain your dignity." He gestured to the bench seat.

Caitlin glowered at him, but did as he'd suggested and climbed back onto the bench. "You see what I'm up against?"

He needed a beer. He went to the small fridge next to the sink.

"So, you'll help me?"

He bent and snagged one of the beers he kept on hand for moments exactly like this. He really, really hated to be told what to do. Especially by a guy like Ian Neisson.

Bodie straightened and turned to meet Caitlin's striking blue eyes. Thank goodness she'd washed that damn blue tear off. "No, princess. I won't."

CHAPTER FOUR

C AITLIN STOOD IN the deep shadows of the competitors' RVs, watching intently for Plan C to make an appearance. Plan A—talking Alec out of riding bulls—had failed miserably, as had Plan B—securing Bodie Hadley's help. She dearly hoped she wouldn't have to exhaust any more of the alphabet to keep Alec safe, as she'd promised her mother she would.

And knowing Ian was hunting around for her was not going to make finding help any easier.

Whatever letter she landed on wouldn't be any easier with Ian on her trail. To think, he'd actually knocked on Bodie Hadley's door looking for her. It was as if Ian had a sixth sense when it came to sniffing out any and all shenanigans she might be up to. Only what she was trying to accomplish tonight far outweighed anything she'd tried to get away with as a kid.

She shivered and hugged herself tightly against the cold night air as the temperature rapidly dropped. A reliable feature of the high desert. She'd been so focused on finding Bodie, she hadn't grabbed a jacket. Tilting her head back, Caitlin stared up at the crystal-clear night sky blanketed by a seemingly endless number of stars. Even the lighting scattered around the rodeo grounds couldn't obscure the amazing display put on by the night sky over Pineville. Unfortunately, she was strung too tight to enjoy the view.

She probably should wait until morning to approach Josh Caldwell with her request, especially when there was a very good chance she was even further off base than she'd been by asking Bodie. But she didn't have the luxury of waiting. She was running out of time. And Josh was literally the next best thing to Bodie on the bull riding circuit. At least he had been until Bodie quit competing. Josh had gone from always a bridesmaid to the star of the show.

It was rumored that the only reason he was in Pineville now for this regional rodeo was that, after suffering an elbow injury on the national tour, he needed to test how well he was recovering. A bold decision. Sure, the bulls here weren't as intense as the bulls leading the Bull of the Year race on the national tour, but they'd still do a number on any rider not at the top of his game.

Riders such as her brother Alec, who had no game at all where bulls were concerned.

Injured or not, Josh Caldwell, who she'd seen pressing the flesh at the sponsors' party, was her best hope for getting the help she and Alec needed. Especially if she let slip Bodie Hadley was dead set against what they wanted to do.

It was common knowledge that Bodie and Josh had been beefing since their days on the tour together. Most riders were friendly with, even supportive of, their fellow riders, going as far as helping each other in the chutes. But not

Bodie and Josh. They were two very competitive men who'd, at some point in their careers, rubbed each other the wrong way.

The sound of two men talking as they walked toward Caitlin's hiding spot had her stepping backward, deeper into the darkness between two RVs. She had no idea what Josh sounded like, but she knew she'd waited in the right spot. The RV on her left was decorated with a larger-than-life photo of the man in question. Humble was not an adjective ever used to describe Josh Caldwell. Plus, he had a talent agent who knew a thing or two about branding and publicity.

The men drew closer, entering the glow from a nearby lamp. The taller of the two men was the one speaking.

"She told me I was better lookin' in person than my big ol' picture, professionally taken and all. Of course, I had no choice but to agree with her."

Definitely not humble.

The other man laughed, then gestured toward the decal-sporting RV. "Is she waiting for you in your rig?"

Caitlin grimaced. She hadn't considered the fact that Josh might have scored female companionship at the party earlier in the evening. Though he probably didn't need a party of any sort to meet and woo women. Professionally taken photos or not, the man was easy on the eyes.

"Nah. The only date for me tonight is with a bucket and a bag of ice. I need to soak the elbow."

"That's right. You need to take care of that thing."

Caitlin shook her head at the serious note in the other

guy's voice. Plenty of riders competed with freshly broken bones or recent surgeries. But few had the sort of endorsement deals that Josh Caldwell had, where his physical appearance was just as valuable as his bull riding abilities.

As the men drew closer, she could clearly see that Josh was the taller guy, and even in the dim light, how good-looking he was.

Not as good-looking as Bodie, though.

The thought entered her mind unbidden. She rolled her eyes at her own silliness. Bodie may be better looking, but he was also a Hadley. Enough said.

Josh clapped his left hand on his companion's denim jacket-clad shoulder, and Caitlin noticed Josh was, indeed, favoring his right elbow. He held his right hand just above his large silver belt buckle, a casual enough position, except for the way he kept that elbow tucked tight against his body. Maybe he was still seriously injured.

Yet here he was competing at a regional rodeo. Caitlin shook her head again, this time at the choices some of these guys made.

Josh said, "So this is where I leave you, my friend."

"See you tomorrow, man."

Both men tipped their cowboy hats to each other in farewell, and the shorter man continued down the path between the larger RVs. Josh turned toward his RV and dug a set of keys from the front pocket of his jeans.

Not wanting to risk Josh having lied about having a woman waiting in his trailer—hey, it could happen—Caitlin launched herself from her hiding place in the shadows. "Josh

Caldwell?"

Josh reared back away from his RV and clutched at his chest with his good hand, leaving the keys dangling from the lock. "Jesusmaryjoseph, you startled me."

Caitlin stopped in her tracks. Maybe this wasn't the best way, or time, to do this. But if not now, when?

She raised a gentling hand and eased toward him. "I'm sorry. I didn't mean to scare you. My name is Caitlin, and I was hoping you had the time to speak with me for a moment."

As she drew closer and further into the light, his entire demeanor changed. He straightened to his full height and squared his shoulders. Not to show he'd recovered from being startled, but rather what a fine specimen of rugged, desirable maleness.

Great, just what she needed, another Rodeo Romeo. Maybe that's actually what he and Bodie had beefed over. Not who was the best rider on the circuit, but who was the best with the ladies.

Definitely Bodie.

She sighed and tucked her hands into her back pockets.

Josh's gaze dropped to her chest, and she yanked her hands from behind her and clasped them in front instead.

He raised his attention to her eyes and smiled. "I'll always have time for you, darlin'."

"Caitlin." This time, she offered him her hand.

He looked at it and hesitated. He was right-handed. How was he supposed to anchor himself to a tornado in bull form with an arm he couldn't even extend for a handshake?

She yanked her hand back. "I'm sorry. Again."

He waved her off. With his left hand. "Don't worry about it. It's nice to meet you, Caitlin. I'm Josh."

She laughed. Definitely not so smooth. "I know." She suddenly realized how exposed she was. If her oldest brother was on the hunt for her, which he would be until he found her, the last place she should be was standing in the glow of a portable streetlight talking to another bull rider. Knowing she only had one real option, she gestured toward his RV. "Can we talk?"

His hesitation this time was much, much shorter. "Yeah, of course. Definitely." He resumed unlocking the door and swung it open for her. "After you."

"Thank you." She smiled up at him and noticed in the light spilling from the RV that he had the most remarkable light hazel eyes. Not hard, steely gray, but warm and tempting, like melting caramel. She turned to mount the steps into the RV and tripped on the first step. Why wasn't any of this easy?

"Whoa, careful there, dumplin'."

"Caitlin." She grabbed the handrail and managed to get up the short stairwell into Josh's rig. She was instantly overwhelmed by the overabundant use of mahogany and flat-screen TVs. Clearly Josh was doing well for himself. A glass-fronted, built-in trophy cabinet full of glinting silver championship buckles and trophies removed any doubt.

The RV door clicked shut and Josh came up behind her. "Have a seat anywhere you like."

Being considerably wider than Bodie's fifth wheel and

double the size of the trailer her family had towed the short distance to this rodeo, she had the choice of a long narrow couch, the bench around the dinette, and the captain's chairs in the front. She chose the dinette bench. Just on the off-chance Ian came banging on the door here and she needed to dive for cover under Josh's table.

"Can I get you something to drink? A beer? Soda? Sparkling water?"

She shook off each offer. "No, I'm fine. Thank you."

He arched a chestnut brown eyebrow at her beneath his hat. "Just talk?"

Caitlin calmly folded her hands on the table—actual wood, not white and gray-speckled Formica—and noted in the back of her mind that her palms were not sweating. "Yes."

"Okay." Eyeing her speculatively, he removed his hat and began to unbutton his red and blue-striped, long-sleeved collared shirt.

She unclasped her hands and slipped them into her lap. So much for dry palms.

He worked his way down his shirt, revealing a white undershirt beneath. She realized she'd been holding her breath when it escaped her in a rush.

Shrugging his good arm out of his sleeve and using it to ease his injured elbow free of the long sleeve, he said, "You look really familiar. Should I know you?"

"You probably know one of my—" he turned slightly and she was stopped by the sight of the angry red surgical scar running along the back of his elbow from mid-triceps to halfway down his forearm. The joint itself was swollen significantly.

Oh no. What if, because he'd suffered an obviously serious injury, he had the same reaction as Bodie to what she wanted to do? What could possibly be Plan D?

She shifted on the bench seat, but the soft suede upholstery didn't make a sound. "Um, you might know one of my brothers or maybe my cousins."

He reached into a lower cupboard, which turned out to be a mini-freezer, and pulled out a bag of ice. From the sink, he lifted a large plastic bowl and set it on the table. He ripped open the bag of ice and dumped as much of it as would fit into the bowl. Taking a seat opposite her, he eased his bad elbow into the ice with a hiss. "Sorry, babe, but that does not narrow it down."

"Caitlin."

He looked up from adjusting the chunks of ice around his elbow. "What?"

"My name is Caitlin." Not darlin', dumplin', or babe. "Caitlin Neisson."

"Ah. You're Thomas Wright's granddaughter."

The way he said it made her feel like she was twelve again.

"I've been picking Wright bulls whenever possible, ever since I made it to the big leagues. Good bulls." He flexed his fingers and nodded as if a great mystery had been solved.

"I wanted to ask you a favor."

Both his eyebrows went up this time.

She tried to remember what she'd said to Bodie, but

could only remember his bulging muscles and how his body heat had radiated off him. And the fire and electricity that had coursed through her when they'd kissed. She would never forget the sensation. He'd taken up all the space around her and filled her head with the scent of spice, horse, and man.

"Which is?" Josh asked.

Caitlin forced herself to focus. "I need your help. My brother wants to ride bulls, but he doesn't know anything—well, not enough—and I need to learn how to bullfight so I can keep him safe."

Josh stared at her for a moment with those remarkable hazel eyes of his, then barked out a laugh. "That's a good one." He shook the index finger of his good hand at her. "You almost had me for a second. But really, what can I do for you? Sign some promo stuff?"

Caitlin shook her head and opened her mouth to tell him no, but he'd shifted his attention to readjusting his elbow in the bowl.

"I'll tell you up front, I can't sign many." He looked up at her and waggled his right fingers, which were rapidly paling from the ice bath. "I'm right-handed. But only while writing or riding. With everything else, I'm very ambidextrous." He winked.

She shook her head again, partly to convey her meaning and partly to free herself from the charm trap he was tossing her way. He might not be a Hadley, but he was a top bull rider on tour. With a huge picture of himself stuck to the side of this RV. Not her type. "No, no. I don't want you to sign anything. I promise." She leaned forward to stress how serious she was. "And this isn't a prank of any kind. My brother Alec and I need your help."

His eyebrows dropped and he pulled in a breath, but she cut him off before he could speak.

"Look, you're tall. Alec is tall. You lanky guys have to ride differently than the other men. You could help him with that. And with the amount of experience you have, you could also teach him how to study the bulls he draws so he won't get killed on his first out."

"Sticking to the back of the bull is the best way to keep from being killed. Or avoiding bull riding completely."

Her frustration returning, she looked toward the closed wooden blinds on the window above the eating area and muttered, "That's practically what Bodie said."

Josh straightened in his seat. "Bodie? As in Bodie Hadley?"

"Yes." She hadn't really wanted to invoke the specter of whatever had been, or still was, going on between Josh and Bodie. But if she'd been willing to use her feminine wiles to get Bodie to talk to her, she certainly couldn't balk at stirring up a little male rivalry.

"You asked *that* guy." His voice had raised an octave. "*That* guy." He paused and lifted his elbow out of the ice bath, sending melting ice and water sloshing all over the table. She made a wall with her hand to stop the mess from ending up in her lap.

Keeping his dripping elbow bent, he pointed in the unnervingly accurate direction of Bodie's fifth wheel. "Before you asked me?"

Dang. She hadn't considered that she might be called out on her plan. She shrugged and willed away the heated flush growing in her cheeks. "Well…he has his own bulls. Bulls without horns."

Josh scoffed and reached for the forest green dish towel hanging from a knob on the cabinet across from them. He carefully dabbed the water from his injured arm. Again, Caitlin was struck by the improbability of his elbow being capable of providing him an anchor on the back of a bucking bull.

"He told you no?"

More like, *Over my dead body*. There was no point in hedging. "Yes."

"Did he say why?"

"Not exactly."

Josh nodded, as if he had no problem imagining Bodie's refusal to communicate. "Well, it doesn't take a mind reader to guess why he doesn't want to be the one to put your brother on a bull and you in the arena."

Guilt flashed through Caitlin. He wasn't wrong. And she'd played dirty in her attempt to secure Bodie's help.

Josh tossed the dish towel onto the counter. "He wouldn't have been much help to either you or your brother, you know."

The image of Bodie, completely at ease atop his big gelding, orchestrating his men with nothing more than a lift of his chin, and keeping several tons worth of bull from decimating downtown Pineville, flashed in her mind. "How so?"

"He's handicapped," Josh said with a dismissive shrug.

"What?" Caitlin had a permanent impression of Bodie's tall, strong body pressed against hers. There was nothing wrong with the man.

"He has to be. What other explanation is there?" Josh slid from the seat and, with his left hand, picked up the bowl of ice. As he turned and dumped the ice into the sink, he continued over the loud clatter of ice on steel, "I mean, the whole point of being a bull rider is to prove nothing can keep you down." Josh looked at her over his shoulder. "Bodie's still down." Josh shrugged and resumed his seat, his right arm tucked tight to his side.

"Bodie was gored—"

"Doing his job."

"And my cousin was killed."

"Doing *his* job. A job I know he loved." He leveled a hard look at her that turned his eyes nearly gold.

Caitlin dropped her gaze to the table top as a flush of embarrassment heated her cheeks. Of course, Josh had known Charlie. They might have even been friends. Sometimes it was easy to forget her family members had lives separate from the Wright Ranch.

"Besides," Josh added, "no one likes Bodie."

She thought of the extra two coffee cups drying on the edge of Bodie's sink. His men seemed to like him. Unable to prove it, she inanely countered, "His horse likes him." Her brother Ian always said a person could judge a man by whether or not his horse liked him. Ian's horse loved him, and Caitlin couldn't think of a better man than her eldest brother. But Ian also kept apple maple oat treats in his pocket for his horse, so who knows.

Josh made a disparaging noise and waved off her measure of a man. "I'm guessing what happened to Charlie is why your remaining bullfighting cousins and those brothers of yours aren't helping you, instead."

"They keep saying they're going to help, but they don't. Even though my dad said I could do what I wanted. But I don't think he believes I'll really do it. He doesn't know about Alec, though. None of them would be happy about both of us being in the arena with bucking bulls."

"And neither would Bodie." Josh cupped his elbow and she could practically hear the wheels turning in his head.

"No. Bodie is not happy about the idea."

Josh grinned the way Liam did when someone had dared him to do something. Like Bodie, Josh had a gorgeous smile, but her pulse and temperature didn't spike the way it did when Bodie smiled at her.

Instead, the hair on Caitlin's arm stood up. *Uh-oh.*

Josh rapped the knuckles of his good hand on the table. "In that case, my answer is yes. I'll help you."

THE SUN HAD yet to crest the eastern horizon when Bodie made the rounds of his bull pens. His breath misted the air and the single cup of coffee he'd downed did nothing to dispel the cobwebs created by a sleepless night.

Boomerang had upended his water trough and had one

side of his metal pole pen knocked askew. The huge Brahman bull behaved like a giant toddler.

A giant toddler who loved to have his ear scratched.

Bodie indulged his prized bull with a good ear scratching through the rails until Boomerang started pushing his considerable weight against the gate. Bodie gave him a pat and a hearty shove. The bull blew out a wet huff and backed up. Bodie was unfastening the gate so he could right the trough when he heard voices approaching.

"Just do as I say, Neissons, and you two will be in Vegas at the Nationals in no time."

Josh Caldwell. Bodie didn't have to look to know who was the clueless idiot giving the two Neisson siblings advice. He'd know that arrogant, fake drawl anywhere. The guy was from Idaho, for crap's sake. Josh Caldwell was the personification of everything Bodie used to be until reality had stuck a horn in him.

"Remember, Alec, just wait for the jumps and have fun."

"Got it. No problem."

Just wait for the jumps and have fun? What kind of coaching was that? Telling a bull rider to wait for the jumps and have fun was like telling a NASCAR driver to just hit the gas and turn left. What was Josh thinking?

"And you, darlin'—"

"Caitlin."

"Yeah, I know. You just make sure you don't get caught flat-footed."

"Got it. No problem."

Oh HELL no. Bodie gripped the top rail. That woman

and her sarcasm. And her stubbornness. Caitlin was going to get herself and her brother killed.

Bodie realized with a flash of certainty he didn't have the strength to carry any more guilt.

CHAPTER FIVE

B ODIE READJUSTED HIS grip on the top rail of Boomerang's pen, stretched his arms out and dropped his head
down between them as far as he could without knocking his
hat off. His breath, heavy with frustration, formed a white
cloud in the cold morning air, obscuring his cowboy boots
and the light, loose soil of the bull pens.

"Excellent," Josh said. "I think we're off to a great start."

Anger swamped Bodie. As much as he wanted to keep
the maximum distance humanly possible between himself
and anyone connected to the Neissons or Old Man Wright,
there was no way he could stand for this. Not only was
Caitlin stubbornly going ahead with a plan he'd told her in
no uncertain terms was dangerous, he couldn't allow Caitlin
to turn to Josh Caldwell for help. No matter how he might
admire her determination, the anger and resentment he felt
toward Josh and an unexpected surge of protectiveness for
Caitlin overwhelmed his better judgement. No way was this
happening.

Pushing off from the pen with a clack of metal, Bodie
turned and hooked his thumbs into his belt, all casual like, to
hide his agitation.

The noise he'd made had caught Caitlin's attention, as he intended, and she turned toward him. Today, she looked the epitome of a successful rancher, from her black wide-brimmed cowboy hat, a tan canvas barn jacket, dark-wash jeans, and well-worn boots. She'd plaited her silky blond into a braid down her back, and her blue eyes sparkled even in the pre-dawn gloom. Her steps faltered.

He greeted her with a quick hitch of his chin. "Morning."

Caitlin stopped dead, a deer in his headlights.

Josh and Alec stopped also, silencing their spurs. Josh squared his shoulders and faced Bodie, ready for battle. Bodie's suspicion about why Josh had agreed to help Caitlin and Alec was immediately confirmed. Caitlin must have admitted to Josh she'd asked for Bodie's help first.

Alec just looked confused, glancing between his sister, Bodie, and Josh.

Josh recovered first, having years of experience in verbal—and nonverbal—warfare with Bodie. "Mornin', Hadley."

"Kinda early for a tour of your trophy cabinet, ain't it, Caldwell?"

Josh glanced down at Caitlin and puffed up his chest. "Never too early to show a pretty girl my big buckles."

Alec looked at Josh as if he wasn't sure if he should puke or punch him.

Caitlin rolled her eyes and pushed aside her jacket to plant a hand on her jean-clad hip. Beneath the coat she only wore a red, waffle-weave Henley shirt. She wasn't dressed to be out in the arena with a bull. At least Alec had on leather chaps and a black, protective vest over his heavy, dark jeans and light-gray hoodie. He was also carrying a black, cage-masked helmet in his hands.

If only a vest and helmet could save a man from horns and hooves.

Caitlin leveled an I-have-four-brothers-and-I'm-still-the-princess look at him and said, "Josh is going to help us."

"No, he's not." It was all Bodie could do not to snarl the words. She would end up hurt learning anything about bulls from Josh, as certainly as she would if she'd asked Bodie before his wreck.

Josh interjected, "Yes, I—"

"Because I am," Bodie cut him off. He looked right into Caitlin's sky blue eyes and said firmly, "You asked me first because you know me and my bulls are the best for the job."

Caitlin stared back at him long enough to make him want to fidget, but then a slow, satisfied smile spread across her lovely face.

He felt it smack in the middle of his scarred chest. He'd been played.

She said, "I'm going to hold you to that, Hadley."

Damn.

IT WAS ALL Caitlin could do not to jump up and down and crow. She hadn't intended for Bodie to catch them with Josh like this, because in no way had she believed Bodie would change his mind. But now that he had decided—actually demanded—to be the one to teach her and Alec, she was nearly beside herself with relief.

Josh's cavalier attitude about what she and her brother were about to do had created a sick, sinking feeling in her stomach that had been growing by the second. Last night, he'd insisted she and Alec wear their regular clothes to avoid suspicion—and interference—from the rest of their family, but, thankfully, Alec knew enough not to climb on a bull without protective gear.

Actually, nothing seemed to worry Josh. Despite the morning chill, he'd left his RV without a coat when she and Alec had fetched him. Probably because he wouldn't have been able to get any sort of outerwear on over the heavy-duty, hinged contraption he had on his injured elbow. The black, padded neoprene and metal brace encased his arm—his bull rope arm—from wrist to upper biceps. How much help could he give Alec in the chute? And so far, the only topic of conversation Josh seemed interested in revolved around a certain local girl both he and Alec were acquainted with.

Men.

Josh handed off to Alec the heavily-rosined bull rope he was loaning him, then he squared off with Bodie. "Don't you have some bullshit to shovel, Hadley?"

Bodie smirked. "Only if you keep talking, Caldwell."

Alec snorted in amusement. Leave it to a brother of hers to appreciate a well-executed verbal slam. All the Neisson boys could turn pro if it were a sport.

Josh ignored the jab. "Look, I have them handled. I'd already arranged to do a practice ride on Big Blue this morning, but Alec can give him a go, instead."

Bodie nodded sagely. "Saving that busted-up elbow of yours a world of hurt as a side bonus."

Caitlin shot Josh a look at the same time Alec did. Thinking she'd misheard the bull's name, she said, "Wait, what?"

Alec said, "Big Blue?"

Josh shrugged. "Yeah, Big Blue. He's a great bull."

Bodie visibly bristled. "If you're a top-ten ranked rider."

"Which is why I was going to warm up on him," Josh shot back.

Regaining her wits, Caitlin said, "No, you were going to put my brother on him. Big Blue? That bull has been consistently scoring in the forties all year. And he likes to turn to the left, away from Alec's rope hand."

Josh, Bodie and even her brother gawked at her.

"What?" She spread her hands. "Like a girl can't know bulls. And I'm not just talking about my grandfather's."

Alec pulled his chin back, probably because he knew she'd avoided any and all bulls since her and their mom's accident. She'd been studying, though. Enough to know Big Blue was not the bull for Alec to cut his teeth on.

Bodie grinned at her the same way he had when she'd been dressed as a clown. A tingling warmth rippled through her, and the memory of his lips on hers flashed in her brain.

Caitlin rolled her eyes at her own foolishness. She needed to push the memory of his kiss aside once and for all. She could never be romantically involved with a Hadley. Her grandfather wouldn't stand for it. If this collaboration with Bodie was ever going to work—and she needed it to work—she had to get a handle on her attraction to him.

Fast.

And she couldn't let him know how scared she was about what she and Alec were about to do.

BODIE WATCHED CAITLIN roll her eyes in a whole-body way that men were incapable of.

Damn, she was something.

Something in a beautiful-and-stubborn-incredibly-attractive way.

Caitlin heaved a sigh and looked at the three men as if they all spent too much time at the wrong end of these bulls. "Where did I grow up? A rough stock ranch," she said to Josh, as if he didn't know, which he did. Every bull rider knew of her grandfather and his family. "Of course I know a thing or two about bulls."

Alec interjected, "Yeah, but you haven't gone near them since you and Mom—"

"I agree with Caitlin," Bodie cut Alec off. No one should be reminded of an incident like what Caitlin and her mother experienced. Especially by her brother. Bodie met Josh's hazel gaze. "Big Blue is no bull for a complete novice to climb on."

"I'm not a novice," Alec objected.

Caitlin's blond brows shot up. "Excuse me? What bulls have you ridden? And don't you dare say Buckaroo Bonsai. Even I can stay on B.B. for eight seconds."

Alec huffed in exasperation, banging the bucking rope against his leg.

"Buckaroo Bonsai?" As a former bull rider and current breeder of rodeo bucking bulls, Bodie prided himself on knowing the competition, and he'd never heard of the bull.

Caitlin shifted her annoyance to him. It wasn't quite as adorable when directed at him. "That's what we named the bucking barrel Ian strung up between the trees behind the old barn at home."

Now this surprised Bodie. "Ian wanted to bull ride?"

"Before he grew a brain," she retorted.

Josh barked a laugh, and Bodie fought to suppress a grin as he nodded his complete understanding.

Only Alec appeared insulted. "What makes you think I want his help?" He gestured toward Bodie with his helmet. "He killed Charlie."

The kid was not wrong.

Caitlin gaped at her brother. "Bodie did *not*. No one killed Charlie. He was doing his job. A job he loved." She sent Josh a look Bodie didn't like at all; a look of respect. Shifting those cloudless-sky eyes at Bodie, she continued, "Charlie died in an accident. An accident that wasn't Charlie's fault or Porky Chop's fault." Her gaze drilled into his. "Or Bodie's fault."

Just as he had the day of the parade, Bodie found himself falling into her eyes. Only this time, the sensation was worse, because he knew what she felt like in his arms, how she tasted. But if he was going to keep her and her brother safe, he had to remain objective.

Alec clearly wasn't having any of his sister's rationalizations, shaking his head adamantly. "Everyone knew that bull was dangerous, and when he started whooping it up instead of getting clear—"

Caitlin cut her brother off. "The bull was in the line-up." Meaning she knew Porky Chops had been chosen to compete.

"I would have picked him," Josh said quietly. Then more loudly, "If I could have. But Bodie had a better time than I did going into the championship round. If he hadn't beat me to it, I would have picked Porky Chops. He was carrying a ton of points. Everyone pretends otherwise, but the points were worth the risk on that bull. And I sure as hell would have celebrated my ass off if I'd stuck to him for eight."

Bodie could only stare at Josh. Not even Bodie's own family had ever voiced such words of support. For those words to come now, from his most reliable rival, was almost too much to handle. Fortunately, Bodie had grown a spine of steel from bearing the weight of his guilt from that day.

His throat was nevertheless too tight to speak. Bodie could only give Josh a nod in acknowledgment of what his admission meant to Bodie.

To Caitlin and Alec, Josh said, "And on that revealing and humiliating confession, I'll leave y'all to it. Besides, my agent wants me drama free, if you know what I mean." He gave a tug on the brim of his cowboy hat. "Big Blue awaits."

Alec held out the bull rope Josh had loaned him, but Josh waved him off.

"I have others. I'll get it back before I leave town after the rodeo," Josh said, then turned and sauntered off.

Despite Bodie's newfound respect for his longtime nemesis, he reached a hand out to Alec. "Let me see that rope."

Alec hesitated a moment, then with obvious reluctance handed over the bull rope so Bodie could inspect it. The handle was American style, with a smaller opening for the rider to thread his hand through. Brazilians had introduced a larger handle that cut down on hang-ups, and the long tail of the rope wrapped the opposite way around the bull.

Bodie looked up at Alec. "You prepared to wrap your pinkie?" To keep the American-style rope from slipping to the side of the bull, riders often wrapped the tail of the rope through at least one finger. Usually the pinkie. It was a great way to get hung-up on a bull and leave the arena with a busted finger, but the rope wouldn't slip.

Alec shrugged as only a nineteen-year-old male can. "I can ride however."

Bodie gave Caitlin's brother a hard look. Alec didn't so much as blink.

Bodie reminded himself that all the Neisson children had grown up under the roof of Thomas Wright. Being glared at had to be a daily occurrence.

"Alrighty then." Bodie handed the bull rope back to Alec. "Let's get you a *however* bull." He turned and started walking toward his other bull pens. Boomerang ranked right up there with Big Blue when it came to suitability for a novice.

Behind him, he heard Alec grumble, "We don't need him. *Especially* not him."

"Yes, we do," Caitlin hissed back. "His bulls are perfect. And I doubt there will be any rampaging bulls breaking loose with him around. Safety is important to him."

"A little late."

Bodie continued walking as if he couldn't hear them, but he had to pull in a lung-full of the crisp morning air to dislodge the grip regret had on his chest. He looked for any sign of Danny and Cabe around the pens. They should be back from the ranch with the horses. He'd need Cabe to help him with Alec in the chute. And while he wasn't going to let Caitlin into the arena dressed as she was, when the time did come for her to face her first bull in the arena—if she actually went through with it—there was no one he'd trust to be out there with her more than Danny.

No way could he do it himself. He should, but he couldn't.

"Look," Caitlin said softly to her brother. "I know this is hard. And, trust me, the only reason I'd associate with him is because he can provide what we need. He can help me learn what I need to do on the ground in the arena, and he has the safest bulls for you to ride before you try competing."

So much for her words of support. It was all Bodie could do not to turn around and ask her if she considered nibbling on his neck *associating* with him.

Fortunately, they'd reached the temporary pen holding the bull he knew would be perfect for both Alec and Caitlin's first go-around. He stopped and turned to face the siblings trailing in his wake. "Meet Bit O' Honey."

He stuck his hand through the metal rails of the pen and, as he knew would happen, the curly, golden-haired bull immediately came to him and ran his long, slobbery tongue the length of Bodie's palm. "Be warned, he's a kisser, but he also loves to buck."

Alec came right up to the pen so he could scratch the swirl of short curls on the wide space between Bit's big brown eyes. "He's not very tall." Alec was clearly trying to disparage Bodie's bull, but the smile tugging at his mouth said he was falling under Bit's spell.

Bodie did his damnedest to breed for good temperament, but Bit O' Honey was the bovine equivalent of a golden retriever.

Caitlin hung back, her hands buried deep in the pockets of her barn jacket, her shoulders up and anxiety plain on her beautiful face.

Bodie scratched his bull's cheek. "Yeah, he's short, but his stature is another reason he's perfect for you. Tall riders can have trouble with smaller bulls. And there are plenty of these little fireplugs on the circuit." He gave Bit a good ear scratch. "It's best to figure out your technique with them from the get-go." Bodie turned so he could catch Caitlin's troubled gaze. "Plus, this guy will turn himself inside out to keep from stepping on you."

His reassurance didn't clear the clouds from her blue eyes. The last thing he was going to do was pressure her. Especially when he'd prefer she abandon her plan completely.

She visibly gulped. "What's the best way to distract him?"

So much for her abandoning her plan. "We'll get to that later. You're not dressed for the arena today."

Caitlin looked down at herself and nodded. "I know. Just give me a minute." She turned on her heel and headed toward the trailers.

"We'll be in the arena," Alec called after his sister.

She raised a hand in acknowledgment but didn't stop. Her long blond braid danced behind her beneath her black hat as she broke into a trot and disappeared around an RV.

"Starting the day with a little sugar from our Honey?" Danny said from right beside Bodie. He was holding the leads of Bodie's horse, Dutch, and Danny's roan mare, Bebe, who stood patiently behind him, saddled and ready. Danny practically vibrated with curiosity as he looked between Bodie and Alec.

Bodie hadn't noticed their arrival. With one last glance at the spot where Caitlin had disappeared, he said, "We're holding an impromptu bull-riding lesson. Bit O' Honey is on board. Do you have time to lend a hand?"

Danny's eyebrows disappeared beneath his hat as he pointed at Alec.

Bodie nodded. "Yep. Alec Neisson is going to be a bull rider. And his sister has it in her head to learn to bullfight. She'll be joining us *in a minute*, apparently. We're going to make sure they get off to a good start."

Danny blinked at him. "Didn't see that coming, but

okay. Count me in."

Alec heaved a sigh. "Can we just do this? The less time I spend with you, the better."

Bodie couldn't agree more. "You heard the man." Bodie lifted Bit's halter and lead off the gate latch and entered the pen. The good-natured bull made it easy for Bodie to fasten his halter on and lead him out of the pen. "Where's Cabe?"

"He's coming."

"Good. I'd like his help too."

Danny reached into the breast pocket of his fleece-lined denim coat and produced his cell phone. "I'll text him to meet us at the chutes."

"Thanks. Oh, and tell him to bring a flank strap." Bodie said and started their procession toward the Pineville Rodeo's arena.

Bit O' Honey placidly followed Bodie, and they arrived at the entrance to the chutes without incident. With the sun barely beginning its ascent over the eastern horizon, the grounds were still mostly deserted, but that wouldn't last. As Alec had said, they needed to do this.

Big Blue was pacing in the holding pen, butting his head against the vertical gate to the chutes. Like Bit, Blue loved his job. But unlike Bodie's bulls, Blue brought foot-long forward-curving horns and a very bad attitude to the office. Alec's step faltered at the sight of the huge bull with enough gray in his black coat that he appeared blue.

Yep, dodged a bullet by not having to ride that one first, kid.

There was no sign of Josh or the stock contractor's rep

for Big Blue. Good. Bodie didn't want to have to explain what they were doing to anyone else.

Cabe clanked his way down the metal stairs leading to the platform above the chutes, the requested flank strap looped over his shoulder. "What's up, boss?"

Bodie opened another gate to the chutes and unclipped Bit O' Honey's lead from his halter. "Just an impromptu bull riding clinic for Alec, here."

"Alec *Neisson*?" Cabe practically squeaked.

"Yep. Can you help us by handling the flank strap on Bit while I show Alec how to mount without getting himself stacked up?" Bodie handed the lead rope to Danny so he could use it to pull the chute's gate into the arena open.

"*Show?*" Cabe and Danny asked simultaneously.

"Tell. I'm going to *tell* him how to do it," Bodie corrected himself. No way would he ever sit a bull again. Not even a sweetheart of a bull like Bit O' Honey.

Relief that their world hadn't suddenly been knocked off its axis washed over his guys' faces. They definitely knew him well.

Cabe nodded. "Right. Sure, I can help." He pivoted and went back up the stairs.

With nothing more than a gesture, Bodie sent Bit O' Honey through the gate that would funnel him to the chutes. Using the same gesture, he urged Alec to proceed him up the stairs and onto the platform. Bodie gave the kid points for only hesitating for a heartbeat. The guy apparently really did want to do this.

Good bull that he was, Bit had trotted through to the

last chute, and Cabe lowered the gate behind him before looping the soft cotton rope just in front of Bit's considerable junk. Danny had hustled into the arena and wrapped the lead rope around a bar on the gate so he could swing it open when Alec gave his nod.

Bodie was in the process of showing Alec how to wrap the bull rope just behind Bit's shoulders when he heard Danny say, "Hey…whoa, Caitlin?"

"Morning."

Bodie straightened away from the chute and looked down into the arena. His breath froze in his chest.

Caitlin stood a few feet behind Danny kitted out in what had to be one of her cousins'—God help him if it was one of Charlie's—bullfighting gear, complete with protective vest beneath an oversized red jersey, matching padded shorts and shin guards under knee-high white socks. She even had on cleats and a red baseball cap through which she'd threaded her long blond braid.

Bodie's heart started to pound and he broke out in a cold sweat.

It was as though he'd been transported back in time.

To the very worst moment in his life.

"I can't do this," he said and headed for the stairs.

CHAPTER SIX

JOSH HAD WARNED Caitlin to never get caught flat-footed in the arena. And that was exactly what happened to her when Bodie had laid eyes on her, declared he wouldn't—no, that wasn't right, he *couldn't*—do what he'd promised and left the chute platform. Stunned, she'd simply stood there, as flat-footed as a duck, staring at him as he stormed off, disappearing from the arena.

"Caitlin, you okay?" One of Bodie's guys asked as he approached her.

She realized her mouth was hanging open, and she closed it with a snap of her teeth. "I'm fine, um..."

"Danny. Danny Kline." He extended a hand to her when he reached her.

Blushing in embarrassment, she shook his hand, realizing too late her palms had been sweating. "Nice to meet you, Danny." He had the warmest dark brown eyes and a welcoming smile. But her focus was still on Bodie. What just happened?

"And that's Cabe McBride up there with your brother." Danny gestured up at Bodie's other ranch hand on the platform with Alec. "Don't know if you're acquainted or not."

She shook her head. "No. So thanks." Caitlin shifted her gaze back to the spot Bodie had disappeared from her view. "Is Bodie okay?"

Danny hooked his thumbs in his front jeans pockets and considered the top of the stairs where Bodie had literally fled. "Yeah," he breathed out. "Bodie is a tough son of a gun. Toughest I know, actually." He returned his attention to her, his gazed running the length of her. "But do you realize how much you look like Charlie in that gear?"

Her jaw dropped again as the ramifications of the outfit she'd donned slammed into her. "Oh, geez. Oh, *hell*. I didn't even consider—" She looked down at the jersey. Despite the fact the equipment smelled to high heaven, she remembered how good, how *right*, she'd felt after she put it on. Especially with the name Neisson emblazoned across the back.

She met Danny's sympathetic gaze. "It's not Charlie's, I swear. My dad and uncle packed up his things and— actually, I don't know what they did with them." She fingered the edge of the sponsor's logo sewn onto the chest of the red jersey. "This is J.D.'s gear. Except for the socks and cleats, of course. I raided the kit locker he'd left in the main barn's tack room. He's away at college right now and won't be using it. He won't mind." At least she hoped he wouldn't. Plus, her youngest cousin was the closest of the boys to her in stature.

Charlie had been just a little taller and lankier.

She put her hands to her face as regret washed over her.

"You sure do look the part, though," Danny offered.

A part she'd never play if she didn't find someone to help her. She let her hands fall to her sides and looked at Danny. Before she could completely form the thought, he shook his head and brought his hands up as if to ward her off.

"Oh no. Not me. I like my job and I want to keep it. Also, I went to school with Liam. I like being alive too."

Caitlin blew out a breath. So much for Plan D. "It's okay. I get it." Then something else, something awful, struck her. "Did Bodie go to school with Charlie?"

Danny shook his head. "No. Charlie was a year behind. But they were friendly—as friendly as a Neisson and a Hadley could be, I suppose—because of their work. They were both fast approaching the top of their games, so...yeah." Danny petered off, his discomfort with the subject obvious.

The sick feeling grew in Caitlin's stomach. She shifted her gaze back to where Bodie had disappeared. She had to fix this. She needed to make Plan B work. Hopefully it wouldn't go the way of Plan A, which had been talking Alec out of trying his hand at bull riding. Alec wasn't about to budge on his decision. "Where do you think Bodie went?"

Danny hesitated.

"I have to apologize to him, Danny. I didn't consider how this—" she waved a hand at her getup, "would affect him."

Danny readjusted his brown cowboy hat and looked toward the chutes and the platform above them where Cabe was still talking with Alec. Hopefully Cabe knew a thing or two about bull riding, as well as the bulls themselves, and was sharing his knowledge with her little brother so this morning wouldn't be a complete bust. Bit O' Honey had wedged his muzzle against the bars of the chute gate to the arena and was blowing loud, snotty huffs at her and Danny as if he was annoyed at not being allowed to do his job.

Finally, Danny hitched a thumb at the big black gelding dozing next to his roan on the other side of the arena railing. "Dutch is still where I tied him, so Bodie probably went back to the fifth wheel. Or he might be with our bulls. Probably Boomerang's pen. That bull needs a babysitter."

Hope surged through Caitlin again. "I know which bull that is. Thank you, Danny." She touched the sleeve of his jean jacket, then something else occurred to her. If Danny had gone to school with Liam, he had to have been in the same class as Charlie too. Her heart constricted, and she wrapped her hand around his muscled forearm. When he looked down at it, she gently squeezed. "I'm sorry about the gear."

He met her gaze, his brown eyes darkening with loss. "Charlie was a good dude. But don't worry about me. I'm okay. Go talk to Bodie."

Caitlin gave his arm one last squeeze, this time in gratitude, before releasing him and taking off at a run for the nearest exit out of the arena.

"Cait!" Alec called after her from up on the platform.

She waved him off, then yanked the gate open. "I'll text you later," she yelled back and shut the gate with a clang.

"Caitlin!" her brother hollered, but she didn't stop.

She did, however, slow down enough to peel J.D.'s jersey

and baseball hat off. The last thing she wanted to do was make anyone else believe they were seeing a ghost. When she'd changed, she'd kept her thermal Henley on beneath the protective vest, not just because the vest smelled, but because the newly risen sun hadn't put a dent in the morning chill yet.

Caitlin reached the bull pens first. Boomerang was using his nose to push his already overturned trough around the pen. Danny was right, he needed a babysitter. There was no sign of Bodie. She continued on to his fifth wheel. As far as she could tell, there were no lights on inside the RV. But all the blinds were drawn, so she couldn't be sure. She glanced around to see if anyone was watching, especially her two oldest brothers. The coast was clear. After switching J.D.'s hat and wadded-up jersey to her other hand, she reached up and knocked on the metal door.

Silence.

She knocked again, harder this time.

Nothing.

There were a dozen other places he could be, but—his reputation aside—there was something about Bodie that made Caitlin doubt he'd go where there were other people right now. He must be inside the RV.

She stepped up onto the folding steps and gently tried the knob. It turned. He either hadn't locked the door when he'd left or he was inside, ignoring her. There was only one way to find out.

She turned the knob again, then pulled the fifth wheel's door open slightly. No lights were on inside, but she could smell freshly brewed coffee. She thought of the three coffee mugs next to the sink that she'd noticed the night before and hesitated. He could have left the door open so his men would be able to come in whenever they wanted and have a cup of hot coffee.

Again, there was only one way to find out.

Caitlin gingerly stepped up into the RV as silently as she could while wearing her new cleats and closed the door softly behind her. She stayed in front of the door for a moment, listening for any sound Bodie might make and allowing her eyes to adjust to the dimness inside the trailer. All she could hear was her own pounding heartbeat.

Her eyes adjusted and she could see that the space in front of the sink and cooktop was empty. So was the bench around the Formica table. The seating area beyond was occupied only by the spare tack and bull ropes.

She glanced back toward the front of the RV and realized the pocket door separating the bedroom from the rest of the RV was only half-closed. It was too dark to make out any details beyond the door. Gritting her teeth, she eased closer. The small light of the coffee machine on the counter glowed red, indicating the coffee in the mostly-full carafe would be hot. There were now only two coffee cups on the tea towel next to the empty sink. He'd had a cup, but his men hadn't, yet.

Hopefully Alec and Bit O' Honey would keep them occupied until she changed Bodie's mind.

Closer now to the two shallow steps leading up to the partially open pocket door, Caitlin realized she could make out the foot of the bed within the dark bedroom. As well as a pair of jeans-clad legs stretched out on top of the bedspread. A familiar pair of boots had been set on the floor, one upright and the other tipped over.

Bodie.

She froze. Bodie was here, in his RV, in the dark. Not out taking care of his bulls on which his future success in the rough stock business depended. She had literally sent a grown man who'd once made a living sticking to the backs of bucking bulls to his bed. How could she ever fix this?

"Just get your coffee and go."

He'd heard her, but assumed she was one of his men. She reflexively took a step back.

One leg on the bed shifted, bent at the knee. He wore bright red socks. She had no idea why, but the sight of his socks had her regaining her step. Then taking another, onto the stairs. And another, until she stood at the entrance to the bedroom with one hand on the doorframe of the pocket door he hadn't closed completely and the other still holding J.D.'s jersey.

She looked in at Bodie, laying on top of the bedspread with an arm thrown over his eyes, and her heart pinched in her chest. What had she done? He still had his jacket on and his cowboy hat rested on his stomach. His poor stomach.

He flung his arm off his face and straight out onto the bed with a huff. His hat was knocked to the side. "What?"

Her throat was so tight she could barely speak. "I'm so sorry, Bodie."

He jerked upright, knocking his hat to the floor.

She automatically slipped into the bedroom and retrieved his hat.

"What the hell, Caitlin?"

"I had to say I'm sorry for wearing this—" She raised his hat first, then realized her mistake and switched and lifted her other hand holding the red jersey she'd initially been so proud of.

He heaved a soul-weary sigh and swung his legs over the edge of the bed, his gaze on the parquet floor between his red socks.

Afraid she was blowing her chance to fix her mistake and regain Bodie's help, she started talking fast, "This isn't Charlie's gear. I swear on my family. It's J.D.'s. He's my youngest cousin, and he's away at school, so he's not using it, and it didn't even occur to me that it might remind you of...of—"

He'd shifted his gaze to hers, and the pain, regret, and guilt in his turbulent gray eyes stole her breath.

"Oh, Bodie—"

"Don't, Caitlin. Just don't."

She had to.

Before he could kick her out, she quickly sat on the bed next to him. She was careful to tuck the offending jersey and baseball hat behind her out of his view. Just to be safe, she placed his cowboy hat on top of them.

He shifted his gaze from her and continued to stare at the floor.

Everything rational in her told her not to, but something more base, more instinctual, had her reaching out and touching him, molding her hand over the rounded cap of his shoulder. The heaviness of the burden he couldn't put down was right there beneath her palm.

As was the heat of him. He radiated warmth like the brightest of sunbeams.

She started to slide her hand away, but he reached across his chest and covered her hand with his, pinning her hand to his shoulder. His palm was rough against the back of her hand. She sat still and silent as the air around them grew heavy with anticipation.

But he didn't move again and kept his gaze on the floor.

Unsure what to do, she studied his handsome profile, how his short but thick dark beard accented the line of his jaw, how there was a small bump on the bridge of his nose she hadn't noticed before. His long black eyelashes were thick, as were his eyebrows, a dark slash across his furrowed brow. The hair on his head, equally as dark, was thicker still. And at the moment stood on end.

"You have hat hair already," she said inanely.

He slid her a look and dropped his hand back to his lap. "Why are you here, Caitlin?"

Her cheeks heated, and she quickly removed her hand from his shoulder. "To apologize."

"For what?"

She raised her eyebrows at him and gestured at the black protective vest, ridiculously long padded shorts hanging over her knees and the cleats dirtying his bedroom floor. Dang. She should have taken them off.

He heaved another chest-expanding breath and shook his

head. "You have nothing to apologize for."

"Clearly, I do. I should have thought—"

"No. No one should have to think about what he or she says or does around me. Especially you. I've impacted enough lives already. Especially yours."

Frustration bubbling up inside her, she twisted her seat and brought one knee up onto the bed so she could more fully face him. "Your wreck was an accident, Bodie. Charlie's death was an accident."

"If I hadn't insisted on riding that bull—"

"Then someone else would have picked him from the pool. Someone like Josh. You heard him. He said as much. And he also said he would have celebrated like you did if he'd stayed on for the full eight seconds. If you hadn't picked that bull, then he would have. And Porky Chop might have gone after him, and Charlie would have still protected him."

Bodie looked her in the eye, and the tempest of pain in his gray gaze caused her throat to squeeze tight. Slowly and succinctly he said, "Charlie is dead because of me, Caitlin. No one else. Me."

The backs of her own eyes started to burn, and she dropped her gaze. There was a thread coming loose on the top of the knee-high socks she was wearing over J.D.'s shin guards, and she began plucking at it. "I know what it feels like to be responsible for someone else's death."

"What are you talking about?"

"My mom. What happened to her was my fault."

"Don't be ridiculous. She died because of her injuries. Injuries you didn't give her and couldn't be responsible for.

You were a kid."

"I was fifteen. Blackjack got out because of me."

"How?"

She shook her head. She'd been over what had happened thousands of times in her head—what she could remember, that is. "I must have left a pen gate unlatched or something. But the fact is, I was in the bull barn. I heard my mom in the vault. She sounded angry. I went to go see what was going on. But when my mom saw me, she grabbed me and pulled me out through the empty paddock saying we had to find Grandfather. Then somehow Blackjack was behind us." Caitlin had no words for what had happened next.

She pulled in a shuddering breath. "I had to have left Blackjack's pen open, or unlatched or something when I gave him a treat. It might have taken awhile, but I killed her." The threatening tears grew more insistent. She curled her fingers into her palms and pressed her nails into the skin as hard as she could, trying to use physical pain to distract herself from the painful memories.

He shifted also to face her more fully. "You said you she was angry? Who was she angry with?"

Caitlin shook her head. "I don't know." She shrugged. "I just can't remember. So much of that day is a blur. Why is it that only the horrible parts are crystal clear even ten years later?"

"Caitlin, you didn't kill your mother."

"Just like you didn't kill Charlie."

He opened his mouth, probably to argue.

She cut him off. "But I know what it feels like to be responsible for someone else's death." She brought her argument back to her original point.

He reached for one of her hands and gently pried open the fist she'd made, looking down at the red half-moons her nails had made on her palms. While cradling the back of her hand in one of his, he ran the calloused tips of the fingers of his other hand over the marks as if soothing them away.

She'd intended to lecture him on how he couldn't blame himself for something that was an accident, and tell him that she understood his pain and desire to avoid that pain or anything that triggered it. Ultimately, she'd intended to sooth away his pain. But instead he was soothing hers.

And his incredibly gentle touch on her palm stirred a different kind of desire in her. She looked up into his eyes, and the molten steel she found in his gaze robbed her of the ability to speak.

He shifted his hand until they were palm to palm. The calloused roughness of his hand was surprisingly comforting. Not to mention the heat of him that moved from his palm to hers, up her arm, then deeper to her core.

He slipped his other hand beneath the hem of J.D.'s shorts and touched her knee. She'd planned on wearing athletic compression tights beneath the shorts, not just for warmth, but for protection against the loamy dirt of the arena. But she'd forgotten them when packing her bag. Her mind had been on keeping the bullfighting gear hidden, and she'd forgotten about including the tights, which were her own, like the socks, cleats, and the Henley.

Bodie's bull-roughened hand encountered bare skin. The

spark of sensation would have made Caitlin bolt from the bed if she hadn't been grounded by his other hand atop hers.

His gaze remained locked on hers as he skimmed his hand higher up her thigh beneath the shorts. Gone was the flirty sparkle that had danced in his eyes when she'd first talked to him at the parade. There was nothing superficial about the way he searched her gaze. He sought an answer to an unspoken question. A question she didn't know.

He didn't seem to be asking for permission to touch her. His hand continued its exploration of her thigh.

He lifted his hand from hers and cupped her cheek. "You can't blame yourself for what happened, Caitlin."

She nuzzled into his hand. "You first."

He made a noise deep in his throat. Amusement or frustration? She couldn't tell.

Caitlin decided she didn't care when he leaned forward and kissed her.

His lips were warm, and his beard and mustache surprisingly soft. She lifted a hand and cradled his jaw, then ran her thumb back and forth over his beard.

He deepened the kiss, drawing her closer.

His chest encountered the protective vest instead of her.

Bodie reared back, blinking at the vest, then met her gaze, looking back down at the vest.

She immediately reached for the zipper to get the unfortunate, not to mention untimely, reminder of what had brought her to his room. "I'm sorry, Bodie. It's J.D.'s, I swear—"

He hooked a hand behind her neck, pulled her forward

to him and kissed her again. This time, he tasted like loss and sorrow.

She was the one to pull back now.

Bodie immediately released the back of her neck as if she'd murmured *no*.

Anyone who said Bodie Hadley was a selfish bastard didn't know Bodie Hadley. Caitlin copied Bodie's move and slipped her hand behind his strong neck, automatically sending her fingers into the satiny hair growing at his nape. She slowly eased him closer, but she didn't kiss him. She settled her forehead against his. "I'm sorry," she whispered.

He reached for the two sides of the vest she'd unzipped. "You really need to stop saying that." Then he slid the vest from her shoulders.

CHAPTER SEVEN

A S IT HAD the night before, the electricity arcing between Bodie and Caitlin made him forget about his scarred stomach or the gloom of guilt that made it hard for him to see the difference between true affection and pity.

The one thing he couldn't forget was that her last name was Neisson.

He didn't care.

When her tongue touched his, he didn't care about anything, only the burning need to get closer. She'd set off a firestorm within him. She made him want to allow himself this moment of pleasure with her, no matter how fleeting.

And it would be fleeting. Because even if they both could conquer the specters of their pasts, at the end of the day Caitlin would still be a Neisson and he would still be a Hadley.

And again, right now, he didn't care. As she pressed her forehead against his and he buried his fingers in her silky blond hair, loosening her braid, he didn't care. He didn't care about anything but getting the damn bullfighting gear off her.

He pushed the vest down her arms. The tab on a Velcro

strap along the bottom of the vest caught on the soft cotton of her red Henley shirt. He shifted his attention to fully extracting her from the protective vest.

"Is it just me, or does this thing stink?"

"Oh, no, it stinks," she said emphatically as she held her shirt taut so he could free her. "I'm going to have to ask J.D. if he has some sort of condition."

Bodie couldn't picture this J.D. cousin of hers. He hadn't been invited to the memorial.

No. He wasn't going there. Not right now.

He tossed the vest against the opposite wall. She loosened the laces on her cleats. She popped them off and let them *thunk* onto the floor.

"Huh. Your socks don't stink."

"They're mine, not J.D.'s. The cleats are new."

She kept stressing her youngest cousin's name. She clearly didn't want to make him think of Charlie for any reason.

But he just did.

The wave of anguish and remorse that had earlier blindsided him at the sight of Caitlin wearing bullfighting gear similar to Charlie's hit him again. A sneaker wave with the power to knock him flat. She had better not be taking pity on him. He'd rather she did her damnedest to seduce him into helping her and her brother than suffer her pity.

Caitlin was struggling to lower her knee-high socks over the shin guards. He placed a hand over hers to stop her.

Part of his brain wanted to tell her to pull them back up. The other part wanted her to let him do it himself. He couldn't decide which came from the part of his brain he was supposed to be ignoring.

She looked up into his eyes. Questioning? Or resigned? He supposed the answer didn't matter because he wanted to kiss her again regardless. He wanted to kiss her every single time he looked into those eyes of hers. She drew him to her in a way no other woman ever had.

Which was exactly why he had to put a stop to this now. Before they both did something they'd regret.

Loud knocking—make that banging—on the fifth wheel's door stopped him from explaining, which was good, because he had absolutely no idea what he'd say to her.

Her beautiful clear blue eyes went round. "Who is it?" she whispered.

"Not Danny or Cabe. They'd just come in."

She hissed air through her teeth.

His mood improved considerably because, for reasons he did not wish to examine at the moment, the idea of getting caught in his bedroom with Caitlin Neisson was far more appealing than actually lowering his barriers to her. He raised a brow at her. "Did you lock the door after you came in?"

By way of answer, she scrambled up onto the bed as if she intended to hide behind him. His expression must have shown his skepticism and rising amusement, because she made an almost growling sound in her throat, changed course, and scurried off the bed.

Watching her, he started to chuckle. "I'll take that as a *no, you didn't lock the door when you came in.*"

After snagging the vest from where he'd chucked it, she sent him a *do something* look before she ducked into the tiny bathroom in the corner of the bedroom. She closed herself in with the barest *click* of the bathroom door.

Before he got up to answer the door, he did her the favor of pushing her cleats beneath the bedspread and readjusting his hat that she'd placed on top of what he figured had to be her cousin's jersey.

The banging intensified, so Bodie hollered, "It's open. Come in, already."

He definitely heard a strangled squawk come from behind the flimsy bathroom door that made him grin.

How could one woman run him through such a gamut of emotions in such a short span of time?

Though remaining closed, the bathroom door jolted with a loud *thud*, punctuated by a muffled but very distinct, "Shit."

She must have hit her elbow—Bodie hoped it was just her elbow—as she struggled to put the vest back on. The bathroom was very tiny.

He reached and opened the pocket door and heard through the trailer's door, "Hadley. Hadley, you in there? It's Alec," Alec stage-whispered.

Not Ian. Bodie shouldn't be relieved, because Alec was still another Neisson. But he was relieved—a little—nevertheless. "I said it was open. Come in, Alec."

He heard, "Nooo…" through the bathroom door.

He smiled. She really was adorable.

The trailer door opened as Bodie was grabbing his boots. He sat on the top of the two stairs that led down to the living section of the fifth wheel.

Alec stuck his head in, looking around the dimly lit RV. "Where's Caitlin?"

Bodie pulled his left boot on. "Do you see her?"

His spurs clinking, Alec came the rest of the way into the fifth wheel. "Then where is she? She took off right after you left."

Bodie used the motion of pulling on his right boot to lean back and check to see if the tiny bathroom door was still closed. It was. But he knew Caitlin could hear everything. He looked back at Alec and asked, "Did she say where she was going?"

Alec unzipped his protective vest and planted his hands on his hips. "No. She just said she'd text me."

Bodie stood. "And she hasn't." Because she'd been busy making Bodie nearly lose what little sense he had left. With her mouth and those summer blue sky eyes of hers.

"No, she hasn't. Which it totally not like—" A phone dinged from somewhere on Alec's person.

He reached into the front pocket of the protective vest, where most riders tucked their mouth guards, and withdrew his phone.

Keeping his phone in the front vest pocket was an excellent way to end up with a broken phone. How serious about bull riding could this kid be?

Alec looked at the screen and the tension left his face. "It's from Cait." With a swipe of a finger, he opened the text and read it. "She says to meet her back at the arena."

Bodie wanted to hoot at the woman's quick thinking texting her brother from the bathroom. He slapped a hand on his knee and stood. "Mystery solved." He was really starting to like that girl. But hopefully she wasn't keeping her phone in the same place as her brother.

Bodie hopped down the last step and moved past Alec to retrieve his mug from the sink. He needed more coffee to deal with this bunch.

Alec gestured toward the mug. "What are you doing?"

Bodie thought it obvious as he pulled the half-full carafe from the coffee maker. "Pouring myself a cup of coffee."

"We don't have time. We need to go now."

"I told you, I'm not…" The image of Caitlin flashed in his mind, telling him that what had happened to her cousin hadn't been his fault. And he thought of that blue tear she'd painted at the corner of her eye, passing it off as part of her clown costume. He'd been right to not be fooled by her attempt to make it a happy tear. How could he risk something happening to her?

"Forget it, Hadley." Alec interrupted Bodie's dangerous musings. "We don't want your help, anyway." He turned to the door. "Hopefully I can find Josh—"

"No. Not Josh Caldwell." Bodie heaved a sigh and returned the carafe to the machine and set his mug back in the sink. "He'll get you killed." Bodie was more certain of the fact than he had been when'd he'd seen them all together earlier. Especially now that he knew which bull Josh had planned on starting them out with.

Alec snorted. "And you won't?"

While the jab was earned, Bodie met the younger man's gaze. And didn't blink. "No, I will not." He gestured at the door. "I'll join you at the chutes in a minute." Sending Alec to the arena first would give Bodie time to talk to Caitlin. He had no idea what he would say, but they needed to talk.

Alec crossed his arms over his chest. "I'll wait. Go ahead and do whatever you need to do first."

The only thing Bodie really wanted to *do* was Alec's sister.

But since that clearly wasn't going to happen, he might as well get this over with. "I just have to get my hat."

Apparently satisfied, Alec opened the door and stepped down from the fifth wheel, but he held the door open. He obviously wasn't going to risk Bodie not joining him and locking him out.

Bodie stepped back up into the bedroom and caught Caitlin in the act of creeping from the bathroom. She opened her mouth to speak, but he stopped her with a raised finger to his lips.

She squatted, as if scrunching herself down into a pill-bug ball would make her disappear. Exactly as she'd done beneath his dinette table when Ian had knocked on his door. Apparently, it was her thing.

Fighting the smile that threatened to erupt on his face, Bodie retrieved his cowboy hat from the bed, revealing a wadded-up red jersey and baseball cap.

Yep, she didn't want a ghost between them. If only hiding what had happened to Charlie under a cowboy hat would make it go away.

He met her gaze as she stood and made like a cactus pressed against the wall. The message he sent was *later*.

He didn't stick around for her response.

AT THE *CLICK* of the trailer door closing Caitlin slumped forward, settling her hands on top of her shorts-covered knees and pulling in a deep breath. To be caught in a man's bedroom—and not just any man, but Bodie Hadley's—by one of her brothers was unacceptable. Her heart pounded at the prospect. She'd give Alec and Bodie a few minutes' head start and then she would head to the arena herself.

Sitting on the edge of the bed, she quickly put her cleats back on and rezipped the vest. She put the red ball cap back on to cover her mussed hair—*when had he touched her hair?*—but opted to carry the jersey again. Not only did she want to avoid scaring anyone, she really didn't want to deal with any questions that would certainly come her way if she was seen by someone she knew while wearing bullfighting gear. Admittedly an unrealistic desire considering how busy it always was behind the scenes at a rodeo of any size, but she could still hope.

She left the bedroom, careful not to slip in her cleats on the stairs, and went straight to the door. She did take the time to peek out through the slats of the blinds covering the small window by the door. No one happened to be walking by, so she eased open the trailer door and slipped outside. Tugging the brim of the baseball hat lower on her forehead, she headed toward the arena.

She'd only gone past a few other trailers when a pair of

hands grabbed her by the vest and hauled her into the shadows between an RV and a horse trailer.

She was about to shout and throw an elbow when Alec said from behind her, "Shh, Caitlin. It's me. Look there." He pointed at a group of cowboys standing in a cluster around the corner of the RV opposite the one they were hiding next to. "I just barely dodged them, but Bodie kept walking and they stepped up on him."

There were four of them. She immediately spotted Bodie, standing with faux casualness as one man stood directly in front of him and the other two flanked him. It took her a few beats longer to realize the cowboy facing off with Bodie was her brother, Liam. Even worse, one of the other guys was her oldest cousin, Jack. The third man was a friend of Jack's. Matty or something.

She knew the general consensus in their little group was that Bodie should have paid a higher price for what happened to Charlie. As if nearly dying from a horn to the gut and the end of a career wasn't payment enough.

She reflexively started toward the group, certain Liam was not discussing the weather with Bodie, but Alec yanked her back by her vest into the shadows.

He hissed, "What are you doing? Are you nuts?" He made a gesture at her. "Look at what you're wearing."

She glanced down at the vest, oversized shorts, and cleats. "So? What of it? Jack was the one who told them I could shadow his team. And Liam knows I intend to do this."

"Intending and actually doing are two very different

things. Liam doesn't want you being on the dirt in the arena. He's made his opinion clear. And Jack hasn't exactly stepped up to teach you anything, has he?"

"No. He's always *busy*."

He gestured in clear irritation at their relatives. "Busy helping Liam accost a Hadley. If you let them see you, there will be questions. Questions Liam will insist you answer. Questions that will invariably lead to the mention of a certain someone." Her brother pointed at the *persona non grata* preparing, oh so subtly, to go toe-to-toe with Liam.

Liam's voice went up in volume along with his agitation. He spoke loudly enough that his words reached Caitlin and Alec in their hiding place. "Like hell. You are doing nothing but trying to take away my family's livelihood. Don't you think you've taken enough from us already?"

Liam was *so* out of line. Bodie hadn't taken Charlie away from them. A horrible accident robbed them of her cousin's presence in their lives. Nor was Bodie taking anything away from their family's livelihood. Bodie's bulls were quality buckers and honest competition for Ian and their grandfather. Caitlin surged forward, ready to give Liam a piece of her mind.

Alec held her back again, holding on to her with a hand on the back of the neck of the vest.

"Just stop." Alec gave her a little shake.

"Quit it," she snarled over her shoulder and tried to bat away his hand, but he wouldn't let go. She had no choice but to watch in silent frustration as the confrontation unfolded in front of her.

She watched Liam step into Bodie's space, attempting to crowd him. Bodie didn't budge, even when Liam was practically touching noses with him.

Liam said, "Everyone knows the wrong guy died in that arena."

Behind her, Alec made a noise low in his throat. He obviously agreed with her that Liam was going too far.

The way her family spoke to Bodie, it was a wonder he hadn't decorated her boot with cow poop the second he learned her name.

Fortunately, Bodie didn't appear to be too impressed or perturbed by what Liam was saying to him at the moment. He actually looked bored, as if he'd heard it all before. Which he probably had. What an awful thing to have to live with.

Apparently deciding he wasn't going to get a rise out of Bodie unless he took his accosting to the next level, Liam stepped past Bodie, knocking into him with his shoulder on his way by.

Bodie didn't react. He also ignored whatever it was that Jack said to him before walking away after Liam. Matty silently followed in Jack's wake.

Turning to face where she and Alec were hiding, Bodie tipped his hat to them in a very obvious mock salute.

Okay, she got it. Her family, and those connected to them, didn't think very highly of him.

But she was definitely beginning to. He had more restraint in his little finger than all of her brothers had in each fist.

This time when she started toward Bodie, Alec let her go.

She had to make amends for what Liam and Jack said. Exactly how, she had no idea.

Right on her heels, Alec spoke first, "Yo, that wasn't cool, man. Liam and Jack were totally out of line."

Bodie's gaze remained on her. "Nothing I haven't heard before."

Just as she'd expected. When she reached him, she breathed, "I'm so sorry, Bodie."

"Why are you sorry?"

"Because—"

He waved off her attempt to apologize. "It's not your fault."

She persisted. "Please, Bodie. Promise me you'll forget what those idiots said to you."

He gave her a look of exasperation. "They didn't say anything to me that I don't already know."

Everyone knows the wrong guy died in that arena.

Her heart stuttered. Hopefully knowing and believing were two very different things to Bodie.

He shifted his gaze to Alec. "You still want to do this?"

"Absolutely."

"Then we better get on it. That arena's gonna get nothing but crowded as the day revs up."

Caitlin gaped at Bodie. "You're still going to help us? Even after,"—she waggled the wadded-up jersey at him—"and in spite of that?" She pointed in the direction in which Liam, Jack, and Matty had sauntered off.

One side of his mouth curled upward in a very naughty lopsided grin. "I'm going to help you two *because* of it."

CHAPTER EIGHT

"CLOSE YOUR MOUTH, Cait. You'll catch flies."

"Thanks for the tip, Alec."

A smile tugged at Bodie's mouth as he walked away from Caitlin and Alec, back toward the arena. Why was he finding himself liking two members of a family he knew for certain hated his guts? Probably for the same reason he hadn't moved to Florida and taken up fishing after his accident. Clearly, he was still listening to the part of his brain he'd sworn to ignore.

His phone dinged with the arrival of a text, and he retrieved the phone from his coat pocket. It was from Danny.

Keep Bit in holding pen or bring back?

Keep. On our way. Bodie texted back. Over his shoulder he hollered, "Come along, kids. Daylight's burning." He didn't wait to see if they followed him or not. If they really wanted his help, they would follow.

When he reached the arena, he saw Cabe in the holding pen scratching Bit O' Honey behind the ear beneath his halter. Thankfully he had the flank strap Bodie had left behind flung over his shoulder. Big Blue was no longer in the pen, and Danny was nowhere in sight.

Opening the gate so Bit could move from the pen into the chutes, Bodie asked Cabe, "Where's Danny?"

Cabe hitched his chin at the line of chemical toilets. "The john." As he patted Bit on the rump to start him through the gate, Cabe looked past Bodie and said, "So we really doing this with them?"

Bodie turned and saw Alec and Caitlin approaching behind him. Alec had the borrowed bull rope in one hand and the black helmet in the other. Caitlin was still wearing the red baseball cap and carrying her cousin J.D.'s jersey. What remained of her long blond braid after he'd had his fingers in it swung behind her back. Relief and dread combined in Bodie's system and formed a nightmarish cocktail. A definite recipe for disaster. But apparently the bad decision side of his brain was driving his bus at the moment.

Looking back at Cabe, he answered. "Yep. Or BASE jumping. They both make about as much sense."

Cabe snorted. "Amen to that."

"You still good with helping me above the chute?"

"You bet." Cabe climbed through the bars of the holding pen, lifted his ever-present lasso off a support post, and headed up the stairs to the platform.

Caitlin and Alec arrived at the pen. Bodie gestured for Alec to follow Cabe.

Caitlin started to drape the jersey over one of the platform's cross support poles.

"You should put that on," Bodie told her.

"It's okay, I don't need—"

"Actually, you do." He went to her and lifted the red jersey off the metal pole and straightened it out with a snap of the thick fabric. "Loose clothing throws off a bull's aim. They end up hooking their horns in a shirt instead of flesh."

She clearly blanched. "But your bulls don't have horns."

"That's right, they don't. Unfortunately, you won't always be facing one of my bulls. And the bigger and more colorful you appear, the more likely the bull will go after you and not the cowboy he just bucked into the dirt and knocked silly." He opened the bottom of the jersey and held it up so she could slide her arms and head into it. "All you have to do is be faster than the bull."

She gave him a bemused look as she took the baseball hat off and pinned it between her legs. "Is that all?" She slid her arms into the jersey.

"More or less. I'm putting Danny in the ring with you. I'm sure he'll have more tips for you. He works in the ring with our bulls all the time." Bodie helped her get the jersey on over the protective vest. As she straightened the hem he reached behind her neck and gently pulled her braid out from beneath the jersey. He couldn't help lingering on the silky strands at the braid's end. Everything about her tempted him to touch. And stay.

"Where is Danny?"

He reluctantly released her braid. "Cabe said he went to use the restroom. Assuming he didn't fall in, he'll be here." Bodie glanced at the row of Porta Potties. No sign of Danny. "You can wait here for him, if you like."

She retrieved the baseball cap from where she'd pinned it between her legs and pulled it on her head with a nod.

He turned to climb the stairs to the chute platform but paused. He needed to have her focus one hundred percent on what she was about to do, and not worrying about him. He faced her again, his hands on the stair railing. "And Caitlin?"

She turned her gaze from the line of chemical toilets to look him in the eye. "Yeah?"

"I knew that wasn't Charlie's jersey. His crew usually wore yellow. Or a stylized version of the stars and stripes." He pulled in a deep breath. It had been five years, but thinking about Charlie always yanked Bodie back in time and the puckered scar just below his ribcage was once again the vicious wound that would never, ever heal because his choices had cost another man his life.

Caitlin's eyes darkened and she stepped forward to cover his hands on the metal rail with hers. "Bodie, I'm so, so sor—"

"No." He gathered her hands in his. Her skin was incredibly soft, her bones delicate. Fragile. "You're not saying that anymore, remember?"

She sent him a watery smile. "You first."

He gave her hands a squeeze, then released her and started up the stairs again. "And don't get caught flat-footed in the arena."

Her laughter lifted the weight off him just a little. She knew he was mocking Caldwell.

"Gotcha," she said and opened the gate to the arena.

"I won't send Alec and Bit out of the bucking chute until Danny joins you, okay?"

She turned long enough to mouth *thank you* before entering the arena.

Her gratitude squeezed Bodie's chest like a too-tight cinch strap. He pulled in a deep breath to ease the tightness and mounted the stairs. His bootheels rapped on the platform as he walked to the chute Cabe had sent Bit O' Honey through to. Cabe had already shown Alec how to wrap the bull rope and was coaching him on the best way to climb down onto the bull's back. The kid shouldn't have any problem because Bit looked to be asleep. He was such a mellow bull. But Bodie knew for sure that the *on* switch would be flipped the second he pulled the flank strap snug.

Bodie looked out into the arena in time to see Caitlin take up her position far enough from the chute not to get caught in the bull's explosive exit from the chute, but close enough to intervene if her brother found himself in trouble. Bodie glanced toward the gate into the arena. Still no Danny. No way was he going to let Caitlin face her first bull—well, technically not her first, but the first she faced willingly—all by herself.

His attention was drawn to a commotion in the stock exit where the bulls left the arena after bucking a cowboy off. He was standing too far to the left to see what was happening. A loud clang of metal echoed off the empty stadium seats, and the wide, tall gate, hung with a large sponsor's banner, swung open.

He heard the distinctive sharp buzz of a cattle prod and smelled the acrid stench of burnt hair familiar to any cowboy who'd been around the movement of rodeo stock for any length of time.

Horror exploded through Bodie. He glanced at Cabe and Alec and saw the same emotion reflected on their faces.

Before he could shout a warning to Caitlin, a nearly two-thousand-pound tannish-red Brahman bull with long, upward curved horns charged out of the stock exit into the arena.

Kraken. A bull who always lived up to his name.

Heaven help them, someone had released the Kraken.

Muscles rippled under the bull's tawny hide, and his rope of a tail flicked in clear agitation. There was no doubt in Bodie's mind that the bull had been hit with a cattle prod, and Kraken definitely wasn't happy about it.

It took all of two seconds for Kraken's angry focus to land on Caitlin in her bright red bullfighter jersey, cap, and shorts. Normally the point of the getup.

But Caitlin had been plainly frozen by terror the second Kraken entered the arena.

Not good. Not good at all.

She simply stood rooted to the spot, arms slightly akimbo, as a Brahman bull was about to trample her into pulp. Or, God help him, gore her.

Acting on instinct and a near blinding surge of adrenaline, Bodie scooped up the coiled lasso Cabe had set on the platform and vaulted into the arena. He'd barely hit the loose soil in the arena before he was running toward Kraken and spinning the lasso. Behind him, Alec had started to frantically shout at his sister to run. Run for her life.

Spurred into action by either her brother's shouts or

Kraken's thundering approach, Caitlin feinted left so the bull would change course then dove right out of harm's way. A classic pro bullfighter move. Maybe it *was* in her blood.

But Kraken had stomping peoples' heads in his blood, so Bodie let the lasso fly. The loop of rope blessedly settled over both of Kraken's wicked horns. Bodie immediately wrapped the rope around his forearm and dug his bootheels in the deep arena dirt. There was no way he alone could stop the bull, but he yanked hard on the rope to at least get Kraken's attention.

Instead, all he ended up doing was a little dirt surfing, the lasso rope digging into his arm where he'd wrapped it.

Kraken had his eyes set on Caitlin, and the big, ornery bull wasn't going to stop until he'd run her down. Bodie was nothing more than an irritating fly buzzing around the bull's horns.

Bodie risked a glance at Caitlin. She was clearly terrified, but she scrambled to her feet and sprinted for the arena fence.

Another lasso went sailing past Bodie, thrown by Alec, and caught Kraken's left hind leg, definitely giving the bull a moment's pause. But only a moment. It wasn't until Cabe entered the arena riding Bodie's horse Dutch and added yet another lasso around Kraken's horns that the bull's attention was completely redirected.

Between the three of them, they were able to finally stop Kraken's rampage.

Bodie immediately looked for Caitlin. She was sitting astride the very top metal rail of the arena fence, wide-eyed and winded, but none the worse for her first bullfighting experience. It wasn't what he'd wanted for her, but at least she'd survived.

He wasn't sure he would, though. Now that the immediate danger had passed, Bodie realized how hard and fast his heart was pounding against his ribcage, and his hands began to shake as the adrenaline ebbed from his system. The arm he'd wrapped the lasso around began to burn from where the rope had tightened to the point that it dug into his skin. He'd sworn to never enter a rodeo arena with a horned bull, yet he'd just leapt in without thought.

He glanced back at Caitlin, still riding the top rail. She didn't appear to be willing to move until Kraken had been wrangled out of the arena. Why did she have the power to make him do something he'd vowed to never do, under any circumstance?

Cabe used Dutch's considerable strength and weight to turn the bull back toward the exit chute. With a flick of his wrist, Alec released the lasso he'd thrown from around Kraken's hind leg, but quickly rewound it in case he needed to use it again. Bodie unwound his lasso from his forearm and let it fall to the ground to trail along behind Kraken. Cabe would take care of it.

"Where in God's name did he come from?" Alec came toward Bodie as he finished forming the loop of his lasso.

Bodie shifted his attention to the stock exit gate and the tunnel of metal-pipe fencing that led to the holding chute and pens. Empty. "Hell if I know." His gaze traveled over the surrounding pens, corral, and stands. "But I intend to find out."

Alec said, "Did you see that burn mark on his flank?"

"No. But I did hear a cattle prod being used before he charged out." People were beginning to arrive with stock. Maybe Kraken had broken loose from the SRG's rep, and someone stupidly tried to use a cattle prod to stop the bull. "I should have moved faster." Bodie berated himself.

"Don't think you could have."

Bodie pointed to the lasso Alec held. "That was a hell of a toss. Ever consider competing as a heeler?" He couldn't recall a heeler ever being killed during a rodeo. And it would get Caitlin out of the arena.

Alec snorted. "Where's the fun in that? I want to do something that challenges me."

"You can't get much more challenging than trying to stick to a bull that wants you off," Bodie acquiesced.

"Exactly."

Cabe trotted Dutch back through the tunnel into the arena. When he reached them, he reined Dutch to a stop. "There was no one back there. And Bodie, all the gates were closed."

Not an accident.

The thought erupted in his head. That could be the only explanation. What he didn't know was whether Kraken's release was directed at him for his involvement in Charlie's death, or at Caitlin for coming to him for help.

"What'd I miss?" Danny called down from the platform above the chutes.

"Where were you? You were supposed to be here to help

Caitlin."

"Some joker locked me in the portable toilet."

Cabe asked, "How'd you get out?"

"Did someone else let you out?" Bodie asked. If there was a witness to what happened outside the arena, he wanted to talk to him or her. It could have been the person responsible too.

Danny pulled a silver multi-tool from his belt and held it up. "Luckily, I'm never without this. It comes in handy for extracting oneself from unpleasant places."

When the three of them in the arena failed to laugh or congratulate him, or whatever response he'd been expecting, Danny's expression sobered. He looked to Caitlin, only now starting to climb down from her perch on the outside of the arena, to Bit O' Honey standing patiently in his chute. "Why? What happened?"

Alec told him, "Cait dodged her first bull."

Danny glanced back down at Bit then to them again, clearly confused.

Bodie looked to assure himself Caitlin had, indeed, climbed down outside the arena, then told Danny, "We'll fill you in back at the trailer. Could you let Bit out? He's been standing there long enough."

"Sure." Danny climbed over Bit and made his way down the chute gate. The moment he swung the gate open Bit exploded from the chute with a leap and two twisting bucks.

Bodie chuckled despite the heart-stopping incident they'd just experienced. He checked to see what Alec's reaction was to Bit's bad-ass bucking.

Bodie was pretty sure he heard the kid gulp.

Without a flank strap or a rider to encourage him to keep going, Bit settled, then spotted the men and sauntered over to them. Bodie knew what he was after and stuck his hand in his jacket pocket. He waited until Bit brought his big, slobbery muzzle to Bodie's pocket before he revealed his hand and the maple and rolled-oat treat. The treats were meant for Dutch, but Bit had sniffed them out one day and become addicted.

Alec made a noise. "Are you sure he's the same kind of animal as that monster we just wrestled to a stop?"

Bodie smiled and scratched Bit's face. "It's all in how they're treated."

Cabe snorted and shifted his seat in the saddle. "You could treat Kraken like a kitten and he'd still want to stomp you. Some are just born mean. And some are sweethearts. Right Lil' Bit? Come on, buddy, I'll get you back to your pen." He made kissy noises at the bull to get him to come, which he did.

"Hang on," Alec said. "I'd still like to try my hand at riding him."

Cabe stopped and looked to Bodie.

Bodie was certain about one thing—the Neissons could never be accused of being quitters. He just hoped their stubbornness didn't get them killed.

Bodie said, "That's fine with me. Bit can use the exercise." To Cabe he said, "Go ahead and lead Bit back around to the entrance to the chutes."

Cabe saluted. "You got it, boss." He made clicking

sounds at Bit O' Honey, who was attempting to chew on the bottom of Dutch's swishing tail.

Watching the huge, placid bull follow his horse and Cabe out of the arena calmed Bodie in a way few things could. Finally feeling ready, he turned to search for Caitlin.

If only he had a treat in his pocket that would make everything sunshine and butterflies for her.

She stood on the other side of the arena fence, watching them.

Hopefully she'd stay there. He wouldn't blame her in the slightest if she changed her mind about bullfighting. Kraken certainly had the ability to change a person's mind about the wisdom of being in the arena with him, even on horseback.

But as he continued to learn more about these two particular Neissons, he seriously doubted she'd give up on what she'd set out to do. At least, not willingly.

RESIDUAL TREMORS CONTINUED to wrack Caitlin as she put her other foot on the ground outside the arena. Doubting she could, or should, peel her fingers from the metal fence railing surrounding the arena. She'd been frozen and simply watched as Bodie's man, Cabe, coaxed a very unhappy, very scary bull out of the arena with the help of Bodie's big black gelding.

She honestly had no memory of traveling the distance between where she'd stood in the center of the ring and where she'd ended up perched on the top of the fencing. She did remember the terror she'd felt at the sight of the huge bull with lethal horns as long as her arm charging straight at her.

And the single thought in her brain had been that she was letting her mother down yet again.

Then Alec's shouts to run had penetrated the fear that had frozen her in place and something innate must have taken over. So here she was, her fingers tingling as the fright she'd experienced drained from her.

Replaced by fury.

She'd been so stupid to think there would never be a dangerous bull loose in the arena on Bodie's watch. How could her trust in him been so misplaced?

"Caitlin."

Her nerves still frayed, Caitlin jumped and turned, praying she'd misheard. She hadn't, and she was engulfed by a sense of doom very similar to what she'd experienced when Kraken had zeroed in on her.

"Grandfather."

CHAPTER NINE

"**W**HAT ARE YOU doing here?" Caitlin asked her grandfather.

He was the last person she thought she'd have to worry about running into while she enacted her plan. But here he was, looking every inch the rodeo rough stock ranching mogul.

Despite his age, he'd just turned seventy-eight—Thomas Wright stood as tall and was as fit as ever. She'd always thought him a handsome man, his silver hair and beard thick and well-trimmed. He wore his spotless cream-felt cowboy hat as if he'd been born in it, and his brown suede, western-cut blazer accented his broad shoulders. His dark-washed jeans were crisp and his brown cowboy boots shiny.

And the man didn't miss a thing.

Caitlin fought the urge to glance behind herself to see if Alec, in his brand-new bull riding chaps and spurs, was still talking to Bodie in the center of the arena.

Aside from digging herself a hole and climbing in, there was nothing she could do about her getup and what it so blatantly revealed. The best she could do was shift her position so her grandfather was facing away from the arena.

"If I'm not mistaken, there is about to be a rodeo here." His sharp blue eyes took in her bullfighting gear from her red ball cap down to her cleats in a quick glance. "And our family is in the *rodeo stock business.*" The emphasis he'd placed on his last three words was subtle, but she didn't think she'd imagined it.

Her laugh was too sharp, too loud. This day was not going well.

"While I have every confidence in your eldest brother's ability to secure this pending rough stock contract, a little backup never hurts. Particularly when there's competition."

Namely from the Hadley Cattle Company.

Caitlin gripped the bottom of the jersey to keep herself from shifting her gaze past her grandfather to where Bodie was in the arena. She had no delusions about how Grandfather would react to her and Alec having anything to do with Bodie Hadley.

Her grandfather's gaze traveled over her again. "I see that, despite what your father believes, you are actively pursuing"—he paused and clearly struggled for the right word, then settled for waving a hand at what she was wearing—"whatever this is."

"I am." There wasn't anything else she could say. And he'd just confirmed what she'd concluded at the sponsors' party—her father had been patronizing her when he'd told her to go ahead and train to be a bullfighter. He didn't believe she'd actually go through with her plan.

Grandfather nodded, not appearing the least surprised. He pulled in a chest-expanding breath. "Obviously, because we lost Charlie, I wouldn't have picked bullfighting as a career for you. Yet, because of what happened to you and your mother"—his deep, gruff voice hitched—"and how it changed you, I think this is actually a good thing for you." He took a step toward her and ran a knuckle down her cheek. "I miss you in the bull barn, peanut."

Caitlin's throat closed tight and her vision swam. She couldn't remember the last time he'd called her peanut. She was so used to Ian calling her by the pet name that she'd forgotten it had been her grandfather who'd given her the nickname.

Never having been one for sentimentality, her grandfather didn't wait for her to be able to speak past the swell of regret and longing clogging her throat. He chucked her under her chin. "As I've always told your cousins, have quick feet and you'll be fine." He turned to walk away toward the rodeo administration's office. Over his shoulder, he added, "And stay away from Bodie Hadley. He'll get you killed."

HE'LL GET YOU killed.

Her grandfather's words echoed through Caitlin's brain as she walked back to the arena fence. Thomas Wright's opinion of Bodie was the exact opposite of her original rationalization for seeking out Bodie. She'd believed that Bodie would keep her and Alec safe precisely because of what had happened to Charlie.

But the memory of the huge tawny bull, with those

wicked long horns, drawing a bead on her, and charging straight at her, weakened her knees. How could Bodie have allowed a bull like that to get into the arena? She intended to confront him and find out.

Caitlin had only climbed back up one fence rail, the adrenaline dump and her encounter with her grandfather making her as shaky as a colt, when she realized what was happening in the arena.

Cowboys being cowboys, the guys had gone right back to doing what they'd been doing before the hubbub. Cabe, no longer on horseback, used a rope to pull the gate of chute number four open. Bit O' Honey burst from the chute as he had before, but now someone was riding him.

Her brother Alec. Even wearing the helmet with its face mask and a protective vest, she recognized the man who'd anchored himself to a huge animal, who wanted him off.

Caitlin lost her foothold and slipped down off the fence rail with a teeth-rattling thud. But she didn't take her eyes off bull and rider.

One arm held high, Alec moved with the bull's jumps, kicks, and spins. And Bit O' Honey did jump, kick, and spin. Nowhere near as aggressively as a bull like Big Blue, but definitely enough to give Alec a good ride.

On the platform above the chute, Bodie held up an airhorn and released a blast of sound obviously meant to mimic the loud buzzer that would sound in competition at the end of eight seconds. Bit O' Honey instantly settled, seeming to know his bucking job was over.

Danny, mounted on the roan horse he'd been leading

earlier, rode forward and, after releasing the flank strap, smoothly retrieved Alec from the back of the positively docile bull. Cabe opened the stock exit gate, and Bit trotted through on his own accord. Caitlin assumed they had an open pen waiting for the amazingly well-trained bull.

In equal parts amazed that Alec had stuck to the bull's back for the entire eight seconds and annoyed that Bodie had let him ride without her in the ring as she'd intended, Caitlin squeezed herself through the fence and ran toward her brother.

"You did it, Alec! You stuck for eight seconds! But you should have waited for me."

Bodie hopped down from the platform into the arena. "He stuck for four seconds. Which was plenty for now."

Alec slid off Danny's horse and peeled the helmet off before he accepted Bodie's handshake. "Four? It felt like a half-hour."

Danny said, "Then eight seconds would have felt like an hour."

Cabe chuckled as he came forward to shake Alec's hand also. "That's why it's called the longest eight seconds in sports."

"I don't care. It was a rush." Alec met Caitlin's gaze. "The good kind."

She heaved a sigh as the fear and tension left her. "I wish you'd waited for me."

Bodie bent to scoop up the flank strap from the dirt and began to coil it around his elbow. "That was my call. You didn't need to be in the arena right after your first encounter with the Kraken. Even seasoned cowboys take a beat after looking up that monster's nose."

She pulled her chin back. "The Kraken?"

He hitched his chin toward the exit chute. "Our uninvited guest."

A fresh wave of horror hit Caitlin in the chest. "I know of that bull. He has a very bad reputation."

Bodie's eyes were cold steel. "I'm aware."

"Yet you let him get in the arena. So much for your 'safety first' routine."

The other men started to protest, but Bodie held up a hand. His jaw set, without a word, he took her by the elbow and escorted her into the exit chute.

Caitlin did her best to ignore the heat of his strong hand on her elbow and her body's reaction to the contact. He was, after all, hauling her somewhere to do who knew what. But all she could think about was what that hand had felt like in her hair, on her bare thigh under her shorts, splayed on her back as he drew her closer...

Bodie stopped in front of a pen where a now placid-looking Kraken was being held. He released her arm and pointed at the raised, almost burnt-looking spot on the bull's hind quarter.

Frowning, she stepped closer to the pen. "Is that—did someone use a cattle prod on him?"

"With extreme prejudice," Bodie confirmed grimly.

Caitlin blinked at him. "Why?"

"Because whoever sent Kraken into the arena wanted him angry."

A shudder raced through Caitlin. "Why?" she asked again.

He shrugged in a way that implied he had a few ideas.

"Because of you?"

He shrugged again, this time like he didn't care, but she wasn't convinced. He cared.

Her heart crimped the way it had in his fifth wheel.

There were a lot of people who wished Bodie ill. All she'd have to do was swing a cat to find a likely culprit. "That doesn't exactly narrow the field of suspects, does it?"

"No, it does not."

Another thought occurred to her. "Or it could have nothing to do with you. I was the one in the arena. Maybe whoever used the cattle prod on this poor animal doesn't think a woman should be in the arena unless she's wearing sparkles and fringe."

He quirked a corner of his mouth. "Could be. But how would they know what you were doing?"

"One of my brothers, namely Liam, could have complained to their friends about me wanting to learn to bullfight. Word could have easily spread that way."

He nodded, his lips compressed. "At least the members of my"—he made air quotes with his fingers—"*fan club* are easier to spot."

A very different type of shudder traveled head-to-toe through Caitlin like a lightning strike. She had no idea of who was willing to hurt her to stop her from learning to be a bullfighter.

Bodie slung the flank strap over his shoulder then rubbed

at his face. "Well, at least we accomplished what we'd set out to do today. We now know Alec can sit a bull and you can dodge one. That was an excellent move you made to get out of this monster's path, by the way."

His praise sent a tingling warmth through her. "Thank you." Now that she knew he hadn't been responsible, she felt bad for thinking he'd been to blame. But, if he wasn't, then who was?

She looked into his gray eyes and knew what they were each thinking but neither would say. They both needed to watch their backs.

BODIE WATCHED CAITLIN'S beautiful, expressive face as she processed the fact that someone had purposefully tried to harm her. It took all he had not to gather her to him and assure her everything would be okay, that he would do as he'd promised and keep her safe.

He couldn't.

Not just because he didn't know if he could keep her safe because he didn't know where the threat came from. But he also didn't want to promise her something he might not be able to deliver. Someone had already died because of him.

Someone close to her.

That fact was etched onto his soul, branded onto his body by a rampaging bull. He had no right to promise her anything.

But it didn't stop him from wanting to keep her safe. He

wanted to promise her she had nothing to fear with him close.

He'd be better off taking her back to her trailer and saying goodbye.

If someone was out to hurt him through her, the sooner they parted ways, the better.

She chewed on her lip for a moment before saying, "My grandfather told me to stay away from you."

While Bodie had been thinking Caitlin needed to keep her distance from him since he'd learned who she was, hearing her say as much knocked the wind out of him. He shrugged it off. "Thomas Wright is a smart man."

"He doesn't know you."

"Neither do you."

She tilted her head and stared into his eyes until he wanted to squirm. "I think I'm beginning to."

Bodie's scar started to itch. He moved away from Kraken's pen, from her, and went to the pen where Bit O' Honey waited patiently. Opening the gate, Bodie called for the bull to follow him. As he led Bit to the gate at the opposite end of the exit chute from the arena so he could take him back to his own pen, Bodie said to Caitlin, "Then you should know enough to do as your grandfather says."

She called after him, "Not a chance, Hadley. Not a chance."

CAITLIN THOUGHT ABOUT following Bodie and his sweet

bull, but decided to give him some space. She'd watched him bring his barriers back up as he'd tried to warn her off. She didn't want to risk them becoming impenetrable.

She returned her attention to Kraken, a bull she knew to be owned by S and R Genetics, whose principal shareholder, Grant Williams, was a longtime acquaintance of her grandfather. Someone he didn't mind competing with at all. And a man who would never risk one of his prize bucking bulls just to get back at Bodie or keep a woman out of the bull riding arena.

Her frustration rising at being no closer to figuring out who'd released the Kraken on her, Caitlin left the stock holding area the same way Bodie had and returned to her trailer.

She was so preoccupied by everything that had happened, the fact that the trailer door was unlocked didn't register in her brain. Until she stepped one foot inside and found her oldest brother sitting on the couch that occupied the nose of the trailer.

"Ian," she said inanely.

"Is Alec with you?"

Though she knew he wasn't, she still checked behind her. "No."

"Then I'll deal with him later. Come in and close the door, Caitlin." He looked casual enough with a booted foot propped atop his knee, his cowboy hat on the other knee, and an arm draped along the back of the couch. His tone, however, dripped ice.

For a split second, she thought about turning and making a run for it—she was appropriately dressed, after all—but she dismissed the idea. Ian would run her down, and even though the padded vest she had on would protect her, she didn't care to suffer the humiliation of her big brother tackling her in front of everyone. So she did as she'd been told and came the rest of the way into the trailer and closed the door behind her. Out of habit, she toed off the cleats and set them next to her boots.

Ian waited, his stillness radiating his anger. When she finished with her cleats and faced him, he said, "When I asked you last night what you were up to, you lied to me."

"Yes." Considering what she was wearing, there was no point answering with anything but the truth. She removed the baseball cap, tossed it on the counter, then started freeing her hair from the rapidly disintegrating braid.

"Not even in my worst nightmares would I have dreamed you'd be foolish enough to get in the arena with Kraken, of all bulls. What were you thinking, Caitlin? You could have been killed."

Surprise flashed through her, but she immediately realized she should have known she couldn't hide anything from Ian. He knew everyone, so he basically had eyes everywhere. And she should have known that even though Ian had been away at college when Blackjack trampled Mom, he'd seen the aftermath and was as haunted by it as any of them. But Alec had been right, it was time to face their fears. She opened her mouth to protest, to tell him what had really happened, but Ian cut her off.

"And you went to Bodie Hadley, of all people, for help?

Bodie Hadley? Seriously?"

Anger flared in her. "I wouldn't have if my own family had helped me. And Bodie isn't some bogie man. He's obsessed with safety, and his bulls are good-natured and well trained. I knew they'd be perfect for—" She cut herself off before she mentioned Alec. There was no point in tossing them both in the fire.

"Perfect for what? Our little brother to ride?" He shook his head as if the concept befuddled him. "You are the last person I would have thought would let Alec climb on a bull."

She raised her hands at the fact that Ian knew everything and nothing at the same time. "I didn't *let* Alec do anything. I tried and tried and tried to talk him out of it. And since I couldn't, I'm trying to do everything in my power to make sure he stays as safe as possible." She left out that she'd made a promise she had to keep.

Ian dropped his boot off his knee and leaned forward. "And you thought using the Kraken was safe?"

"No, I did not," she shot back. How could he think her so stupid? Needing to get her anger and frustration under control, Caitlin pulled her hair back into a ponytail then went to the small fridge and grabbed a bottle of water. "Kraken was an uninvited guest," she used Bodie's description.

Ian's blond brows came together. "What do you mean, uninvited guest?"

She took a long draw from the bottle. The cold water did wonders for her nerves. "The plan was for Alec to ride one of

Bodie's bulls, Bit O' Honey, and I would be on the dirt in the arena to help him if he needed it. Bit was the perfect bull for both of us because of his sweet temperament."

"And Alec rode him, I know."

Of course he knew.

"But you? You end up nearly getting killed by Kraken. How did that happen?"

"Someone released Kraken into the arena through the exit chute. After viciously using a cattle prod on him so he'd be good and mad."

Ian jolted to his feet, knocking his hat from his knee to the floor. "Who? And for God's sake, why?"

"No idea. And we don't know."

"We?"

Looking as if he needed it, she retrieved another bottle of water for Ian. "Bodie and me." She tossed him the bottle.

He easily caught it despite his mind clearly being elsewhere. "So Bodie doesn't think it was simply because someone hates his guts?"

"Actually, that was his first guess. But I was the only one in the arena at the time. His man, Danny, who was supposed to be out there with me, had been locked in a portable toilet. Probably by the same person who prodded and released Kraken."

Ian turned the water bottle in his hand the same way he appeared to be turning what she'd told him in his mind. He seemed to reach a conclusion and set the bottle on the counter. He came to her and took a hold of her shoulders. "Listen to me, Caitlin. You have to be careful. No, forget it.

You need to go home." He gave her a tiny shake. "Right now."

"No. Why?"

He sighed in exasperation and released her. Running his hands down his face, he muttered, "I can't believe they'd go after you to get to me."

"What?"

"Nothing. Never mind."

"Ian! What are talking about? Someone went after me because of *you*? What have *you* been up to?"

"Just do as I said and go home, Caitlin. Now." Ian grabbed his hat up off the floor and started toward the door.

Caitlin stared at him in astonishment. Great. She had to add worrying about Ian to her ninety-nine problems.

CHAPTER TEN

"I AN, WAIT!" CAITLIN stopped her brother just as he grabbed the trailer door handle in preparation to leave. "Please tell me why someone would do something so…" she searched for a word that would encompass the horror she'd felt when Kraken had almost reached her "…so *vengeful* to me to get back at you."

Ian's chin dropped to his chest, and he simply stood there long enough that she thought he wouldn't tell her. Then he released the doorknob and stepped away from the door. He faced the windows behind the couch and planted his hands on his hips.

She'd never seen Ian like this. Worried. Scared? Not even with Mom. He was scaring her. Whatever was going on with him really had him tied up in knots. Ian was *never* tied up in knots.

Caitlin set her water bottle down and took a step toward him. "Ian—"

The trailer door burst open, and Amanda literally leapt inside, the white fringes on the sleeve and chest of her baby blue rodeo princess shirt swinging wildly. Her wide-eyed brown gaze immediately landed on Caitlin.

"Caitlin! Thank goodness you're here. You've got to come. Now."

"Amanda, what—?"

"It's Bodie. You have to come help him. The boys— Liam and Jack and Matty—have Bodie cornered and are trying to start some—"

Ian shifted to face Amanda, catching her attention for the first time and she started to stammer.

"—some... Oh, hey, Ian." Amanda gave Ian a princess wave. Her dark brows high, she turned back toward Caitlin and mouthed *holy crap* at her.

"It's okay, Amanda," Caitlin reassured her friend. "Ian knows about me and Bodie."

Well, sort of. The memory of Bodie's mouth on hers sparked heat in Caitlin's cheeks until she feared they would glow. And if her oldest brother ever found out about how she'd smashed herself against the poor guy in her desperation to secure his help, he'd make Kraken look like a happy puppy.

How was she supposed to have known how decent Bodie actually was? How quickly he jumped to help someone? Everyone made him out to be so selfish. Especially her own family.

But from what she'd seen so far, the real Bodie Hadley was the exact opposite of what people said about him.

Amanda practically went limp at Caitlin's reassurance she hadn't let the Hadley out of the bag. "Oh, thank goodness. For a second there, I thought I'd really stuck my foot in it this time."

"No, you're fine, Amanda," Caitlin assured her. "You said the boys have Bodie cornered? Where?"

"Between the first and second rows of horse and stock trailers by the bull pens. I'll show you." She looked encouragingly at both Caitlin and Ian as she turned back toward the open door, obviously eager to stop whatever was about to happen.

Caitlin shifted her attention to Ian, fully expecting him to be just as eager to put a stop to any confrontation involving their brother. Liam had been out of line too often for far too long.

Her expectation must have shown on her face because he started shaking his head. "I have somewhere I have to be. I'm late already." He planted his hat firmly on his head.

Stunned, Caitlin protested, "But Liam and Jack—"

He settled his hat on his head. "They're all grown men. They'll figure it out." He tugged at his hat as he stepped past her friend. "Amanda."

Slack-jawed, Amanda had to visibly compose herself before she could reply. "Ian." She watched him exit the trailer and close the door she'd left open. Then her gaze jumped to Caitlin's. "Wha—?"

Caitlin raised her hands. "Don't ask me." But now she was certain something was going on with Ian. He never passed on a chance to snatch up any of his siblings by the scruff of their neck and give them a good shake if warranted. Particularly after their mother had been injured.

Amanda tucked her chin and pointed at Caitlin. "Wait—what are you wearing?"

Caitlin looked down at herself. "Oh shoot. I need to change." She dashed into the trailer's small bedroom, stripping off the red jersey and padded vest. Through the open door, she said, "It's J.D.'s. I'm borrowing it." She shucked the shorts and yanked on some jeans and a blue and white, light cotton, buttoned shirt.

Amanda appeared in the bedroom door holding Caitlin's dark-brown cowboy boots. "But *why?*"

"Alec decided he wants to be a bull rider. I have to make sure he stays safe." The fact she'd made a promise to their mother to do so hung on the tip of her tongue, but despite how close a friend she considered Amanda to be, she held back. "Aside from talking him out of it completely, the best way I could think of to protect him was to learn how to bullfight myself. Bodie's helping us." After a quick check to make sure she'd buttoned her shirt correctly, Caitlin took her boots from a dumbstruck Amanda. "Thanks."

"But Jack and—"

"No," Caitlin stopped Amanda from arguing that her cousin and his crew would suffice. "Not after Charlie." If they had to worry about keeping Alec safe, they wouldn't be as focused on keeping themselves safe. Plus, her mother had put this on her, not her cousin.

Amanda opened her mouth, then closed it. No one ever knew what to say when Charlie's awful death was evoked.

Caitlin sat on the edge of the double bed and pulled her boots on over the red socks. Too late, she realized she still had the shin guards on beneath the socks, but she didn't want to take the time to remove them. Fortunately, her boots fit over the extra bulk. "Okay, let's go." She was more than ready to have a word or two with her second oldest brother.

They found the men right where Amanda had said they were between the horse trailers. Only Bodie wasn't alone any more. Danny and Cabe were now backing their boss. The two groups of three men stood squared off like the gangs from West Side Story. In cowboy hats. Caitlin fought the urge to snap her fingers to an imaginary beat.

She and Amanda hung back in the shadow of the last trailer in the row.

Caitlin leaned toward Amanda and whispered, "I'm thinking we could use a little backup of our own. Do you know where your crew is?"

"Yeah. I'll go get them. Don't you dare move until I get back."

Caitlin nodded and waved her on her way, but she already knew she wouldn't be staying put. A raging bull? Yeah, that scared her. A bunch of guys wanting to beat on each other because they basically were cheering for different teams? No big deal. Caitlin ate her cereal with that going on around her.

Besides, at this distance she couldn't hear what they were saying to each other. And Liam had started to crowd Bodie again, invading his space until the brims of their cowboy hats were touching.

Bodie didn't step back. Though his posture remained casual as it had earlier, Caitlin wasn't fooled. The hard set of his jaw revealed how angry he was. She'd seen that look when he'd showed her the cattle prod burn on Kraken.

Grown men or not, she knew they weren't going to *figure it out* any time soon.

She quickly fixed her ponytail as best she could and marched into the fray. Okay, maybe a little closer to Bodie because she couldn't help herself.

There was just something about him.

Liam was growling, "Get it through your head, Hadley. You're not welcome here."

Her brother was so intent on being a bully he didn't seem to even notice her.

"Knock it off, Liam." She shoved him in the chest. He glowered down at her, but barely moved. So she shoved him again with both hands until he took a step back.

His voice low, Bodie warned, "Caitlin."

"No. Liam needs to check himself," she said what she'd wanted to say earlier without Alec here to stop her this time. She stepped up on Liam exactly like he'd done to Bodie.

At the center back of her jeans waistband, she felt Bodie's touch. Probably in case he decided he needed to yank her back. But he let her speak.

Aiming her index finger at Liam's nose, she scolded, "You are out of line, Liam. Bodie has as much right to be here as we do. His bulls are quality buckers, horns or no. He's not taking business from Ian and Grandfather. He's offering fair competition that will benefit all of us because the bulls will end up having to be better at what they do."

Liam's eyes narrowed as he looked from her to Bodie and back. "I swear to God, Caitlin—"

She cut him off. "The past is the past." She dropped her hand and shifted her gaze to her cousin Jack. Normally sweet, fun-loving Jack. "And no matter what we do, or how much we wish to, we can't change it."

She looked to Jack's friend Matty to make sure he was getting the message, also. He was staring at her like her ponytail had sprouted a nest of vipers. Good.

Meeting her brother's deep blue gaze again she said, "End of story." She gave him a light *I love you anyway* pat on his strong chest, then turned to face Bodie.

His hand dropped to his side as if he'd never been touching her. His face remained set in hard lines, but there was a definite sparkle of amusement in his gray eyes.

She reached for the hand he'd been planning to yank her from harm's way with and threaded her fingers through his. "You know what? I'm hungry. How about you make me some waffles?"

BODIE CURLED HIS hand around Caitlin's to make sure he had a good enough grip on her in case he needed to move her out of the way. It was time to resin up, because Little Miss Sassy Pants had just buried her spurs in the hottest-tempered resident of the Wright Ranch.

He met Liam's gaze over Caitlin's blond head. While his eyes were a couple shades deeper blue than his sister's, Liam was definitely seeing red. Clearly the thought of Bodie being anywhere near Caitlin, let alone defended by her, deeply offended Liam, and he intended to make Bodie pay for the trespass.

Caitlin tried to tug Bodie away, but he was sure he didn't want to turn his back on Liam Neisson just yet. The Neisson stubbornness definitely wasn't limited to Caitlin and Alec. Liam was a big dog who'd gotten his ruff up, and he didn't appear ready to give up on this fight.

Bodie could feel the tension radiating off Danny and Cabe on either side of him. They were ready to rabble for him, and while he'd been doing his damnedest to avoid the escalation to violence, he was immensely grateful for them.

Bodie had been looking for Kraken's owner's rep when he'd been penned in by the boy band for a second time. He needed to find the person responsible for the big bull to discover exactly how Kraken had ended up charging the wrong way into the arena. And if the man owned a cattle prod.

Fortunately, Danny and Cabe had noticed the other three men following Bodie and, sensing trouble, hustled to have his back. They were absolutely earning their Christmas bonuses this year.

Caitlin tugged on his hand again. "Come on, Bodie. I'm starving."

Liam's lip curled. Definitely a big dog itching for a fight.

A commotion at the end of the row of horse and stock trailers caught everyone's attention. Four of the Butter Babes were heading toward them, laughing and chattering away. Readying for their duties during the rodeo later that day, they all wore matching bedazzled light-blue western shirts with white fringe, dark-wash jeans, and cream cowboy boots and hats.

The brunette in the lead raised her hand. "Oh hey, Caitlin."

"Hey, Amanda. Hey, girls." Caitlin answered brightly.

"Liam!" Amanda squealed in surprise as if he'd just popped up out of the ground in front of her like a sage rat.

The other rodeo princesses joined in by calling out either Liam's, Jack's, or Matty's name. Even Cabe received a shout-out from the rodeo princess he'd been flirting with before the parade. Mary Jo waggled her fingers at Bodie, but she thankfully shifted her focus to Matty. She wasn't a fan of puckered scars any more than he was a fan of pity.

The men found themselves swarmed by long, curled hair, musical voices, and the sweet, floral scent of feminine temptation.

Caitlin's friend Amanda inserted herself between Bodie and Liam much the way Caitlin had. But unlike Caitlin, Amanda's disposition was cheery as she focused her attention solely on Liam. Even as she chastised him for not seeking her out at the sponsors' party.

Caitlin tugged at Bodie's hand again. "Come on, let's go." She even plucked at Danny's sleeve with her free hand. "Come on."

Danny laughed. "Called in the cavalry, eh?"

Caitlin shrugged, one side of her pretty mouth curling upward. "A girl's gotta do what a girl's gotta do."

Danny lifted his gaze to meet Bodie's. "Go. We're good."

The rodeo court had indeed charged in like the cavalry,

scattering the cloud of aggression to the wind, and redirecting the over-abundance of testosterone to what nature had intended it to be used for—garnering the affection of a pretty woman.

Even Cabe had been caught up by the cute, auburn-haired princess.

Caitlin pulled at Bodie's hand again as she eased away from the group. "Bodie..." she pleaded softly.

As much as he would have liked to rub Liam's face in the dirt, he wasn't going to indulge himself with Caitlin around. Bodie gave Danny a quick nod. "Check in, okay?"

Danny saluted him with a couple fingers to the brim of his hat. "Will do."

Bodie walked away with Caitlin toward the other end of the row of horse trailers, keeping her hand tucked in his. He told himself he retained his hold on Caitlin's hand because if he couldn't make Liam eat dirt, Bodie would make him suck on the fact Bodie was getting touchy with his sister.

That her hand felt designed to fit into his was simply a side benefit.

And the idea of being touchy with Caitlin again heated him in a way nothing else ever had.

CAITLIN INHALED DEEPLY, then exhaled long and slow after she and Bodie cleared the last stock trailer in the row. She'd barely breathed at all during the confrontation and her heart had pounded in her chest once she'd inserted herself between

Bodie and her brother. She hadn't been afraid the men would hurt her. Despite being the most hot-headed of all her brothers, Liam would throw himself in front of a stampede before willingly causing her harm. Same with Jack. Caitlin didn't know Matty, but if he was a friend of Jack's, odds were excellent he was a good guy.

What Caitlin had feared enough to freeze the air in her lungs was the barely contained hostility vibrating between the two groups of men. All of them were big and ranch-strong, and if they had decided to lay into each other, there would have been blood for sure. She wouldn't have been able to bear watching Liam and Bodie hurt each other.

As Bodie led her to his fifth wheel, she expected her heart rate to slow back to normal, but the tiny circles Bodie was tracing with his callus-roughened thumb on the back of her hand kept her heart banging in her chest.

Which was ridiculous. He probably didn't even realize he was doing it.

He released her hand to open the trailer door then stepped aside for her to precede him inside. Her heart rate increased rather than decreased. She hadn't planned on returning to his trailer with him. She had only wanted to extract him from her family's determination to exact some sort of retribution against him.

Had he changed his mind about not getting involved further with her? Was she about to experience another round of Bodie's famous—or was it infamous—sexual prowess? And why did she find the possibility so exciting, not terrifying?

Because she wanted to kiss him again, that was why.

Liam wasn't the only one who needed to check himself.

Bodie raised his brow at her hesitation, and not knowing what to say or what else to do, Caitlin stepped up into his travel trailer.

Bodie took the steps behind her. He gestured to the dinette. "Have a seat."

She did as he instructed, sliding onto the faux-leather covered bench. He washed his hands in the kitchen sink then commenced opening and rooting around in the cupboards.

Confused, she asked him, "What are you doing?"

"Making you waffles. What else?"

Mortification flooded Caitlin. Of *course*, he was making her waffles. She'd told him she wanted him to. He was a guy. A smart guy. A good guy. So he was doing what she'd asked him to do. Despite the fact that she was certain he had a million other things he needed to do before the start of the rodeo tonight.

"Bodie, you do not have to make me waffles."

He squatted to better see into one of the lower cabinets. "Actually, I might not be able to. I'm not seeing a waffle iron. I thought for sure we'd put one in here." He shifted on his heels to look up at her. "Will pancakes work?"

"No. No pancakes. No waffles. You don't have to make me anything. I only said I wanted waffles because I needed a reason to get you out of there and that's what popped into my head." Her dad had always made waffles for her mom. Her throat closed at the memory.

He straightened and sat at the dinette across from her.

142

"You didn't need to rescue me, Caitlin."

"I did. Not because you couldn't handle yourself against Liam, or anyone else. I know you could." He'd survived so much already, he had to be the toughest person she knew. "I did it for me. I wouldn't have been able to bear it if you'd had to fight anyone from my family. It's bad enough that I'm making you help me."

He sat back. "You aren't making me help you. I don't do anything I don't want to."

Caitlin instantly thought of him stopping her from removing any more of her clothing when they'd been kissing on his bed. Her lingering embarrassment over mistaking his intentions for bringing her to his trailer had her blurting, "And you didn't want to *do* me."

CHAPTER ELEVEN

B ODIE PRESSED HIS back deeper into his trailer's dinette bench, certain he'd misheard. "What?"

Caitlin blew out a breath in clear exasperation and leaned her elbows on the table. She looked as if she was about to explain a simple thing to an even simpler audience. "You said you don't do anything you don't want to do. And since you stopped what was happening between us in there—" she hitched a thumb at the bedroom door behind her, "I can only assume you didn't want to…you know, *do* me."

Bodie scrubbed his face with his hands. Just when he'd thought this day couldn't get any weirder, he was summarily proven wrong.

"Is it me? Or is it just because I'm a Neisson? Or worse yet, a Wright?"

"Are you kidding me? There is nothing, I repeat, *nothing* wrong with you." Just the opposite. Everything about her was very, very right. "And, while the fact that you're a Neisson and Thomas Wright's granddaughter would be excellent reasons for me to run in the opposite direction, they are not why I stopped what was happening between us." He heaved a sigh. Why couldn't he just let her think she'd hit on the reason for him putting an end to their encounter on his bed?

Because he liked her. He liked her a lot, that's why, and she deserved the truth. Or at least the first layer of it.

Bodie got up from his side of the dinette table and moved to her side, sliding onto the bench next to her. She started to scoot over to give him her spot, but he stopped her by putting an arm around her shoulders. She initially shrunk away from him as if she didn't trust his intentions. "You smell a lot better now," he joked. But he wasn't really joking. She smelled like everything he loved about summer. The flowers, the warmth, the freshness, the rightness of new beginnings.

She relaxed and allowed him to draw her close against him. "No stinky J.D. gear. Though I still have the socks and shin guards on."

"What?" he laughed and leaned back to see under the table. He could have sworn she was wearing cowboy boots.

"When Amanda came to tell me Liam, Jack, and Matty had you cornered, I was in a rush to change and I forgot to take them off."

"Ah. And this Amanda, is she the same one who told you who I was?"

"Yes. She also thinks the boys—my brothers and cousins—will slaughter you if they find out we...well, we didn't, so it doesn't—"

"Right. Back to that." It took everything in Bodie not to scratch at his scarred stomach. "Look, Caitlin, I assure you, in this case, it really *is* me, not you."

The wry amusement faded from her face and she pulled away. He let her go, lifting his arm from around her shoulders. But he didn't move from next to her. Because he didn't want to.

He did, however, want to change the subject. And they had something of deathly importance to talk about. Folding his hands on the table, he asked, "Can you think of anyone who might have a grudge against you? Or more likely, your family?"

She made a disparaging noise. "Have you met my grandfather? I know you've met most of my brothers. They're not the type to lose sleep over offending someone or hurting their feelings." She pulled in a deep breath that lifted her perfect breasts beneath her thin cotton shirt.

He could feel himself losing a few I.Q. points and made himself focus on her face and the topic at hand.

"But truthfully, no, I can't think of anyone specifically who might want to get back at them by hurting me. Ian said something about it having something to do with him, but—" She stopped and shook off the notion. "No, it was probably Ian just being Ian. He'll shoulder the blame for anything if you let him. Especially where I'm concerned."

Bodie nodded. He could believe it. The men in her family did all dote on her. Their princess in a tower of their making. Something Bodie would do well to remember.

She reached to cover his hands with one of hers. "I might not be able to think of anyone who would want to hurt my family, but I can think of plenty who'd want to hurt you."

He caught her fingers between his, and the contact was

ridiculously erotic. He savored the sensation for a moment before he made himself concentrate. "As you pointed out, you were the only one on the dirt in the arena when Kraken was sent through the exit gate."

She tightened her grip on their intertwined hands.

He looked into her eyes, and watched her try to come to terms with what he was suggesting. She blinked away the clouds of fear and uncertainty. She licked her lips and as he watched her tongue run across the delicate skin, he was reminded of the feel of her lips on his, the taste of her kiss, and the way she made the realities of his world disappear.

Her blond brows lowered into a worried line. "Isn't there a chance it was an accident?"

"Normally, I would say there is always a chance." He thought of her assertion that what had happened to him and Charlie had been an accident, not a willful, stupid wreck caused by his foolishness and amended, "Well, not always. But it being an accident was the first thing to pop into my head. Then I found out about Danny being locked in the toilet. As far as Kraken is concerned, we won't know for sure until I can find Kraken's owner's rep and talk to him. That's who I was looking for when the Lost Boys cornered me."

She laughed. "Lost Boys. Good one. Can I borrow it?"

"Absolutely." He raised a hand to catch a strand of silky blond hair that had escaped from her ponytail. Her normally straight hair was wavy from being braided earlier. He slid the strand between his fingers until it caught on his calluses, then he slowly tucked it behind her delicate ear, his fingers drifting along her hairline. The electricity between them grew like a summer storm, but he couldn't make himself drop his hand.

The memory of the feel of her mouth on his had him so haunted, the next thing he knew, he was kissing her again. Or maybe she kissed him. He wasn't sure. He didn't care. He slipped his hand beneath her ponytail to hold her head. Her mouth opened to his and deepened the kiss. She tasted faintly of coffee, and, God help him, longing.

He moved his other hand from beneath hers and slid it around her waist to pull her closer.

Caitlin's hand slipped beneath his shirt and, before he could stop her, skimmed the gnarled ridges of his scarred stomach.

Bodie jerked back from her like he'd been hit with the same cattle prod that had sent Kraken rampaging into the arena. Only he wasn't filled with rage. Shame and regret had him off the dinette bench and grabbing for his cowboy hat and jacket.

Without looking Caitlin in the eye, he said, "You know, Danny and Cabe should have checked in by now. I'm going to see if they're okay."

Then he was out of the fifth wheel like a shot.

CAITLIN JUMPED WHEN Bodie slammed the trailer door behind him. She realized her mouth was hanging open—again—and snapped it shut.

What had just happened? Bodie had kissed her, the same

as before, and she'd kissed him back, the same as before, because really, how could she not? The chemistry between them was off the charts. Combined with what she'd learned about his character in this short time, she had wanted to kiss him. Very much. But the minute she'd tried to touch him…

Understanding hit her like a cow kick to the temple.

She'd touched his scar from when he'd been gored. Bodie was embarrassed by, maybe even ashamed of, his scars.

Caitlin flopped back against the corner of the bench seat. Maybe he believed she'd be repulsed by them. A ridiculous notion. She'd grown up on a rodeo-rough stock ranch, surrounded by rodeo people. Nasty scars were a dime a dozen. An image of Josh Caldwell's scarred elbow came to mind.

Not to mention what had happened to her mother.

Caitlin had definitely seen her share of serious injuries and their resulting scars. Bodie shouldn't be ashamed of the mark Porky Chop had left on his body. Just the opposite. He should be proud of the proof of what he'd survived and the kind of man the experience had made him.

The kind she wanted to know. To kiss. To have in her life.

But maybe he didn't want her in his life.

Was she too much of a reminder of how he'd received the scar? Of who else had been lost when it'd happened? Danny had grown up knowing Liam and Charlie. What if Bodie had too? She honestly didn't know. Though his reaction to seeing her in a Neisson bullfighting jersey said a lot about what his wreck and the resulting aftermath had done to him.

Caitlin's heart ached for him.

And the part of her that wanted him in her life rationalized, if she was too painful of a reminder of what had happened to him and Charlie, then he wouldn't have agreed to help her in the first place. She mentally brushed aside the fact that he'd initially said no and she'd kind of forced his hand by asking Josh. And if he'd really not wanted to be around her but didn't trust someone like Josh to teach her and Alec, he could have handed them off to Danny and Cabe. He clearly trusted them, and they seemed to know enough to be of help.

The only thing Caitlin knew for sure was that she was confused and frustrated by Bodie Hadley's behavior. She pushed herself upright and slid from the bench. She couldn't just sit here and wait for him to return. Though she was tempted. But she really should make sure the guys hadn't ended up in a fight, after all. As she left Bodie's fifth wheel, she decided she also needed to track down Alec to see if he really intended to compete in the bull riding event later this week.

She dearly hoped not. Because staying aboard a bull like Bit O' Honey was one thing, but could he survive a bull like Kraken?

And would she a second time?

AS THE DAY wore on and the rest of the personnel, competitors, and stock arrived for the official beginning of the rodeo that night, Caitlin continued to search for Bodie. To no avail. She did find Alec back at their family's trailer, seated at the dinette with his hand in a bowl of ice past his wrist. His bull rope hand. Very reminiscent of how Josh had iced his elbow. Minus the surgery and nasty scar.

While Alec hadn't been thrown—heck, he'd been lifted off Bit O' Honey's back by Danny—he'd still managed to tweak his wrist. Successfully heel snagging Kraken might have contributed to the soreness and swelling, also. Whatever the cause, he wasn't going to be doing any bull riding for a while.

At least for a day, two at the most. And Caitlin knew they both needed more time to learn and gain experience.

Caitlin sat across from him at the dinette. "I'll repay you the cost of the entry fee if you skip this rodeo."

Alec gave her the same stubborn look he'd given her when she'd tried to talk him out of bull riding completely. "I'm not quitting, Caitlin. Do you have any idea what a rush it was today?"

Remembering the near heart attack she'd experienced when she'd seen the arena exit gate swing open and Kraken charged into the arena, she nodded. "I have an inkling. But I'm not asking you to quit."

His sandy blond brows shot up. "You're not?"

"No, Alec, I'm not. I promise. I'm only asking you to take the time to learn as much as you can and to wait until you are at one hundred percent."

"Will Bodie help?"

"I think he will, but I'll find out for sure. Please trust me, okay?"

"Caitlin?" he asked, his eyes filling with moisture.

"Yeah?" her voice cracked. She couldn't bear to see any of her brothers upset. Especially her baby brother.

"Seeing that huge bull charging straight for you was the second worst moment of my life."

She knew all too well what the worst moment for him had been. She vividly remembered seeing him sitting on the paddock fence when she and their mother had tried to out-run their grandfather's bull.

Her throat tight, she reached across the table and snagged his uninjured hand. She gave his hand a squeeze and cleared her throat. "I know, and I'm sorry, Alec."

He shook off the moment and pulled his hand from hers.

She smiled at him. "I have something else I need to talk to Bodie about, and when I find him, I'll ask him if he'll keep mentoring you, okay?"

"Thanks, Cait."

"You're welcome, Alec."

She stood up from the table and grabbed her barn jacket. When the sun went down on the high desert, the tempera-ture could plummet. "Have you seen Ian, Liam, or Drew?"

"Liam and Drew came in to drop off some fried chicken before they went back to move stock, but I haven't seen Ian."

Her nose twitched. How in the heck had she missed the presence of fried chicken? She set her coat down, spied the takeout container on the counter by the sink, and snagged herself a drumstick. Having not realized how hungry she'd been since Bodie had offered her pancakes in lieu of waffles, she polished it off in no time. "I saw Ian earlier." The fact that he hadn't been back to help with the stock ratcheted up her concern. But he could be with their grandfather. "Grandfather was here too. By here, I mean outside the arena."

Alec yanked his hand out of the ice. "What? When?"

"Right after you guys wrangled Kraken."

Alec blinked at her.

"It's okay. I don't think he saw you."

"But he saw you?"

"Yes. We talked."

Alec's incredulity was obvious. "And?"

She tossed the remains of the drumstick in the garbage. "And he was glad I was going through with my plan to bullfight."

Alec pulled back his chin. "What? Why?"

It was Caitlin's turn to grow misty. "He said he missed me in the bull barn. I guess he figures if I successfully train to bullfight, then I won't be afraid of bulls anymore." Thinking of the terror that had gripped her when Kraken was charging toward her, she shrugged at how monumental a task overcoming her fear would be. "Hopefully, he's right."

"Huh." Alec stuck his hand back in the ice, obviously trying to process what she'd told him. "Huh," he repeated himself.

"Exactly." She dipped into the tiny bathroom and washed her hands and brushed her teeth.

"Are you going to watch the opening of the rodeo?"

"I need to find Bodie first. You staying here tonight?"

"I don't know. Haven't decided yet."

"I have dibs on the bedroom," she said as she pulled on her jacket.

"Yeah, yeah." He waved her off with his uninjured hand.

She opened the trailer door and stepped down. "There're ace bandages in the bathroom cabinet," she called over her shoulder before closing the door.

"I'm fine, Caitlin!" he called loud enough for her to hear through the closed door.

She walked away smiling. Now she just had to find Bodie.

The logical place for him to be right now would be the bull pens. While bull riding didn't start until Wednesday, she'd learned from her friends that he had eight bulls in rotation for this rodeo, and with the noise and crowds increasing steadily, she was certain he'd be keeping a close eye on his livelihood.

As twilight descended, the huge floodlights around the arena kicked on. The smaller, portable lights positioned around the trailers and pens hadn't turned on yet.

Caitlin kept thinking she'd caught a glimpse of Bodie's hat and jacket, or square jaw and dark beard, but within ten feet, she'd know she'd been mistaken. No one else carried themselves or stood the same way Bodie did, like a man who'd been hooked by death's horn but survived.

Then she spotted what she felt certain was Bodie's tan Stetson and canvas jacket among the horse and stock trailers where the boys had squared off, but she was too far away to call out. She hurried to catch up with him as he walked briskly toward the bull pens.

"Bodie!" she yelled, but he didn't slow.

In the fading light, she saw him turn into a funnel chute used for unloading rough stock from their trailers to a holding pen and she broke into a trot, her sole thought being to catch up with him.

"Bodie, wait!" she called again, but she'd lost sight of him.

She entered the funnel chute, but as far as she could tell in the growing darkness, he wasn't there. But that couldn't be. She knew for sure the man she'd been following had entered the chute. "Bodie?" she called out, less certain about who she'd thought she'd seen. "Hello? Is anyone there?"

Then the loud clanging of metal startled her. She spun on her heel in time to see the chute gate behind her dropping downward, closing off the way she'd entered. The entire structure of the metal-railed chute rattled. Caitlin spun in time to see someone clamoring over the chute, from one side to the other.

Her skin prickled the same way it had when the exit gate in the arena had begun to swing open. A very primitive part of her brain screamed at her *you are in danger.*

She didn't have to be told twice.

She turned toward the metal rails on her left and grabbed the cold rail above her head and put one booted foot on the highest rail she could reach to start her climb. She'd barely climbed a foot off the ground when the structure shook again as the gate at the opposite end of the chute lifted.

Loud chuffs and stomps heralded the presence of a bull

almost as dark as the night sky except for the gleam of upward-curled, pointed horns, almost as long as Kraken's, but as white as whale bone. At first, she thought the bull would stay in the paddock and not enter the funnel chute, at least long enough for her to climb the remaining seven feet of metal rungs to the top.

Then she heard the telltale buzz of a cattle prod being activated in the deep shadows next to the gate.

She was done for.

The tone of the buzz changed as it was pressed against the bull's hide and the poor animal bellowed in pain.

Her heart in her throat, Caitlin scrambled to climb faster, but the bull shot into the narrow chute with lightning speed in an attempt to escape the pain inflicted by the prod. She wasn't going to reach the top of the chute in time.

Above her, she heard, "Not where you want to be, Sassy Pants."

CHAPTER TWELVE

A S THE BIG black bull began his charge into the funnel chute, Bodie scrambled up the chute rails, lunged over the top rail and caught Caitlin under the armpits. With strength born of adrenaline and pure panic, he lifted her up and onto the top rail of the chute, clear of the bull's horns, with bare seconds to spare. Caitlin barely squeaked, and swung one leg over the bar so she could straddle the top rail. The moment she'd gained her balance, she threw her arms around his neck and pulled him to her in a cheek-to-cheek hug.

"Thank God, Bodie. You just saved my life."

Anchoring himself with one hand on the top chute rail, he wrapped the other around her. "And lost a couple of years off of mine. What were you doing in there? Some kind of immersion therapy?"

She pulled back and tried to see him in the dark. "No. I'd thought I was following you."

"It wasn't me." The implication of her words sunk in. "Someone led you into the funnel chute?" Bodie jerked his gaze to the gate where the bull had entered and the surrounding area, but it was too dark now to see anything other than shadows and deeper shadows. But he could see that both gates in the chute had been closed. Someone had purposely trapped Caitlin in the chute with a bull. His stomach clenched with anger. And fear. Someone was definitely out to hurt Caitlin.

"Yes." She drew his attention as she continued. "He was wearing a hat and jacket just like yours." Her gazed lifted to his hat and then dropped to his oiled canvas jacket. "Well, the hat was definitely the same, but the jacket was different. Lighter. But it was getting dark."

"I know how dark it was. I was trying to follow you." He'd been going to speak with her when he'd seen her from a distance heading toward the arena. There was no mistaking the smooth motion of her gait, the way her hair swayed.

Her eyes widened. "You were?"

"Yes. I found the guy in charge of Kraken. The bull shouldn't have been out of his pen, let alone charging into the arena. And he claims to not even own a cattle prod."

"Do you believe him?"

Bodie shrugged, then felt the bull catch the toes of his boot with his horn as he backed up in the chute, trying to find a way out. Bodie shifted his feet out of the way. "I don't know. I'd never met the man before." He waited for the bull to move forward again so he couldn't catch them with his horns through the bars, then he said, "Go ahead and climb down." He stepped down a rail and put a hand under her armpit again to steady her. He could feel her body still shaking. His anger started to crowd out the fear that had left a very bad taste in the back of his throat.

When she'd reached the ground outside of the chute, he jumped down next to her.

She threw her arms around his neck again and hugged him tight. He wrapped his arms around her and savored the feel of her body pressed against his. His heart had yet to settle to its normal rhythm, but holding her like this felt right. Stupid, but right.

"You know what, Bodie?" she asked against neck.

"What?"

"You must have the super power of strength, after all, to be able to lift me out of there like that."

Bodie chuckled and squeezed her gently. He knew his ability to lift her out of the chute before the bull reached her was fueled by fear, pure and simple. If he were to lose her, especially to a bull...well, he simply wasn't going to let that happen.

As much as he'd love to try to track down who was doing this to Caitlin, the shudders he felt still wracking her body made him decide to take her to her trailer or the fifth wheel where she'd be safe and he could make sure she really was unharmed.

He eased away from her, but she was reluctant to release him. Considering her past, he couldn't blame her. She'd had two, count 'em, two very nasty bulls try to put her in the dirt today. He'd be a little clingy, too, if he were her.

"Hey, I'm not going anywhere," he reassured her. "But how about we get you somewhere safe. Where do you want to go?" He'd take her home to the Wright Cattle Ranch—synonymous with the seventh ring of hell as far as his family was concerned—if that's what she wanted.

"Your fifth wheel is closest. Is it okay if we go there?"

"Absolutely." Holding her close to his side and keeping one arm wrapped around her back, he started to lead her toward his trailer.

"Wait." She stopped. "What about the bull?"

"What about him?"

"We can't leave him trapped in that chute. And he might have been seriously burned by the cattle prod like Kraken."

He wanted to kiss her. The animal would undoubtedly have severely injured her at best, killed her at worst. But she was nonetheless concerned for its welfare.

"Will you be okay for a second?"

She nodded. "Yes."

He dropped his arm from around her but only took a half a step away. If she wobbled even the tiniest bit, he wasn't going to leave her. Though she wrapped her arms around herself, she stood steady. "Okay. But don't move. This will just take me a moment."

Bodie backed away from her a couple of steps, making sure she was indeed fine without his support, then turned and jogged around the funnel chute to reopen the gate between the chute and the small paddock. The big black bull would be able to back his way into the paddock if he was so inclined. Metal clanged when Bodie raised the gate. The bull huffed and snorted at the sound. There wasn't enough light for Bodie to identify the bull, either by ear tag, brand, or physical features. Nor could he make out any sign of the man who'd led Caitlin into the chute, then prodded the bull into going in with her.

Belatedly, he thought to pull out his phone and use its flashlight function. The moment he shined the light on the bull he recognized it. Nightshade. Owned by the same contractor who owned Kraken, S and R Genetics. Bodie clenched his jaw. Was someone at SRG looking to eliminate the Wright Cattle Ranch from the competition for the rodeo stock contracts by creating another family tragedy? One that would surely bring Old Man Wright to his knees?

Bodie quickly dismissed the idea. The owners of SRG were good people. And they were smart enough not to use their own bulls to do their dirty work. No, whoever was out to harm Caitlin was simply picking the biggest, meanest bulls, who at this rodeo, happened to be owned by SRG.

He used the phone's light to check the bull's flank for any sign of a burn, but the bull's black coat made spotting any burn more difficult than on Kraken. He didn't see any sign of welting, so he assumed the bull hadn't been badly injured. Just pissed off.

Welcome to the club, big guy.

Bodie directed the phone's light around the chute, gate, and when he noticed it, the portable light that was only about ten feet from the paddock. Had it been on, the entire paddock and funnel chute area would have been well lit. Bodie walked toward it and immediately saw the power cord had been disconnected from the power source. Bodie reconnected the cord and after a *click* and a *hum*, the light atop the collapsible pole turned on, bathing the area with light.

Like the incident with Kraken, this near disaster had clearly been premeditated. An icy chill charged down Bodie's spine.

He sent a quick text to Danny and Cabe, who were helping out with the other rough stock until Bodie's bulls were needed, to let them know what had just happened to Caitlin in the funnel chute and ask them to keep their eyes open. Then he pocketed his phone and hustled back to Caitlin.

She was exactly where he'd left her, with her arms still wrapped around herself like she needed a hug.

He automatically gave her one when he reached her.

She melted into his embrace, and Bodie was struck again by how good she felt. How *right*.

He was an idiot.

"Thank you," she breathed against his chest.

Her gratitude was like a kick to the chest and his throat tightened. He kissed the top of her head until he could speak. "Here's hoping Nightshade knows how to put all that beef into reverse."

She pulled away enough that she could look up into his face. "Nightshade?" She looked toward the chute where the black bull was trying to extract a horn from the bars. "That's Nightshade? But he's owned by S and R Genetics. The same as Kraken."

He could tell she was adding the two together and coming up with three just as he had.

"No. No, I don't believe it. Grandfather and Grant Williams have been friends my entire life. And before I was even born. He would never hurt me, or Grandfather through me.

Plus, Mr. Williams, or his partners, wouldn't be stupid enough to use their own bulls."

Bodie nodded. While he didn't know Grant Williams well, he'd met him and was familiar with the man's stellar reputation. "I agree. I think it's more likely whoever is doing this is simply cherry picking the nastiest bulls here. And they both happen to be owned by the same stock contractor."

"But *why?*"

"I don't know, Cait. But I'm not about to allow the third time to be the charm for this rat bastard."

He felt her shudder again.

He released her and, with a hand on the small of her back, started them toward his fifth wheel again. "Maybe you should tell Ian."

"He already knows. Well, he knows about what happened in the arena with Kraken, at least."

"Then where the hell is he?" Bodie would have expected her overprotective eldest brother to be glued to her side after finding out someone had tried to hurt her.

"I have no idea. Something is definitely going on with him. He wasn't even interested when Amanda came to tell us Liam and Jack and Matty were picking a fight with you."

Bodie scoffed. "Maybe he figured four against one would have been unfair odds."

"No. There is something up with him. And it has him worried. Ian doesn't get worried, Bodie. He even suggested Kraken being set loose on me might have something to do with him."

Bodie stopped them at the edge of the row where his

fifth wheel was parked and met her gaze. "Really." Ian being the ultimate target hadn't entered Bodie's mind. "Did you ask him about it?"

"Of course. But he jetted out of our trailer like his bootheels were on fire, claiming he had somewhere he had to be." She shook her head. "Very un-Ian like. I'm worried about him, Bodie."

He rubbed her arm, wanting nothing more than to sooth away the fear in her eyes. "Ian is a big boy. A very big boy. And he's smart. He'll be okay." But if there was even the tiniest chance Ian knew what was going on, Bodie was going to be having a conversation with him.

And it gave Bodie another reason not to turn Caitlin over to her family to protect just yet. A reason he didn't have to rationalize, that is.

He started them toward his fifth wheel again. When they reached it, Bodie was surprised to see the lights on inside. He slowed and slid his arm around Caitlin again to pull her close.

Danny opened the trailer door. He'd changed into the black, heavy cotton, button-down shirt with the Hadley Cattle Co. logo emblazoned across the back and breast pocket, as well logos for the few sponsors Bodie had been able to coax into taking a chance on his bulls. "There you are. Cabe and I were just about to come looking for you."

He stepped down out of the doorway and moved to one side so he could hold the door open for them, the smell of freshly brewed coffee coming with him.

Bodie handed Caitlin up into the trailer before following.

He gave a nod to Cabe, seated at the dinette and also wearing his black Hadley shirt. "I wanted to find out what bull it was this time, and Caitlin wanted to make sure he was okay. He didn't appear to be hurt."

Danny stepped up into the fifth wheel after Bodie and closed the door behind him. "What bull was it?"

"Nightshade."

Cabe whistled.

Danny immediately looked at Caitlin as if to assure himself she really had escaped unscathed. "My God. Kraken, then Nightshade? You sure are getting a trial by fire for your initiation into bull dodging."

"I'm aware," Caitlin replied deadpan.

Cabe asked her as he slid from the dinette bench, "And you're okay? You didn't get hurt?"

"I'm fine. Thanks to Bodie." She glanced at him, her blue eyes filled with what he assumed to be gratitude.

Cabe gestured to the bench he'd just vacated. "Have a seat. I know my knees would be jelly if I'd just been trapped in a chute with Nightshade. Can I get you some coffee?"

Bodie knew for a fact Cabe had been trapped in tighter spaces with bulls far nastier than Nightshade, but he appreciated his men's solicitousness.

"Yes, please," Caitlin said as she took the seat Cabe had offered. She nodded at both when he held up the cream and sugar.

Bodie took off his hat and jacket and hung them up on the wall pegs then accepted a mug of hot black coffee Cabe had poured him. "Thanks."

Caitlin scooted farther down the bench, which was enough of an invitation for him. He sat down beside her and Danny took the seat across the table. Cabe remained standing, pouring himself more coffee. Caitlin wrapped her hands around her mug as if gaining comfort from the warmth it radiated. Thankfully she'd stopped shaking.

Danny said, "So now what? Aside from making sure Caitlin isn't where bulls like Kraken and Nightshade are?"

"Hang on—" Caitlin began to protest, so Bodie put a hand on her jeans-clad knee to stop her.

"No, Danny is right. Until we know who is trying to hurt you and why, you can't take any chances."

Caitlin didn't quite stick out her lip, but she was clearly unhappy about giving up on her bullfighting training.

Cabe leaned his backside against the counter and said, "And because mayhem-by-bull isn't working out for this asshole, he might switch to something else. Something we're not as good at stopping."

Danny nodded heartily in agreement.

Caitlin looked between the three of them. "But what if he's just trying to scare me? Whoever it is has to know you guys can handle any bull he sets loose on me."

Bodie gave her leg a tiny squeeze to let her know he understood she was looking for a less alarming explanation. "You were alone when he set Nightshade on you. If I hadn't noticed you looking around the bull pens and followed you, I wouldn't have been there to help you get out of Nightshade's reach."

Danny said, "And even if he is just trying to scare you,

the way he's going about it is pretty extreme."

"No kidding," Cabe agreed.

Bodie said to Danny, "Back to your question of what now... Obviously we need to stay vigilant. Keep our eyes peeled. This guy—and Caitlin knows it's a man because she followed him thinking it was me—is clearly keeping tabs on her somehow."

"But *why*?" Cabe asked.

Caitlin pointed at Cabe. "Exactly! Why? Why me? Why now?"

Bodie sat back, but kept his hand on her leg. It was all he could do not to turn the contact into a caress. "I think it's safe to say you haven't done anything personally to this guy, so we have to assume his aggressions have something to do with either your family or me."

Danny scratched at his cowboy hat-smashed hair. "That doesn't exactly narrow things down."

"I'm aware," Bodie repeated Caitlin's deadpan answer.

She snorted into her coffee cup as she finally took a drink.

He gave her thigh just the tiniest of rubs, glad she seemed to be recovering from the scare. "And until he makes a move against someone else, or does something to tip us off to his identity, we're not going to know why. All we know is he's a coward who is using these bulls to do his dirty work."

"So far," Danny added darkly.

Bodie might have imagined it, but Caitlin seemed to lean closer to him.

Cabe said, "If you are the ultimate target," he gestured

with his coffee cup toward Bodie, "then he might try to harm our bulls too."

Danny set his coffee cup down. "Which means bull-sitting."

"Maybe we should just load them up and take them back home like we did the horses," Cabe suggested.

Bodie rubbed at his short beard. His bulls were his future, and the whole point of being here was to gain exposure so he'd have a serious chance at gaining the bigger contract with this rodeo association. "No, I think as long as we have eyes on them, they'll be fine." He looked at Caitlin. "Same with you."

Her blond brows shot up. She was probably wondering what else he planned on having on her. Erotic images formed in his head. He certainly didn't lack imagination when it came to Caitlin. His mouth suddenly dry, he took a gulp of coffee.

Cabe straightened away from the counter and dumped the remainder of his coffee out. "Well, I promised I would help with the broncs tonight." He rinsed his cup and set it upside down on the towel. "So that leaves you with the first shift, Danny. Unless you want both of us watching the bulls, Bodie."

"No, go ahead back to the arena." To Danny, Bodie said, "Do you mind taking the first shift while I make sure Caitlin is safe?"

Danny slid out of the dinette. "Not at all." He opened a cupboard and retrieved a thermos and dumped the remainder of his coffee into it, topping the thermos off with coffee from the carafe.

To both his men, Bodie said, "Make sure you have your phones with you, and that they're charged. Call me if anything, and I mean anything, seems off to you."

"Will do, boss," Cabe said as he grabbed his cowboy hat and headed for the door.

Danny tucked the thermos under his arm and snagged his hat and jacket. He'd be harder pressed to keep warm while watching the bulls than Cabe would be wrangling bucking broncos. Settling his hat on his head, Danny sent Bodie a pointed look. "You do the same, okay?"

Bodie acknowledged his concern with a nod. "Will do."

Danny pointed at Caitlin. "And don't let her out of your sight."

"I don't intend to."

CHAPTER THIRTEEN

B ODIE'S BIG, STRONG hand felt like a hot brand on Caitlin's thigh where his gentle touch had crept up from her knee. She remembered the rasp of his calloused fingertips when he'd slipped his hand beneath the hem of the red knit athletic shorts she'd worn earlier. She'd wanted him to slide his hand higher, to extend the caress to her most sensitive skin, but he'd held back. As he was doing now.

Because they had more pressing concerns than daring to explore whatever it was that was growing between them. Someone had tried to cause her harm. Twice.

Normally she would have chafed at so much male over-protectiveness. She'd been swimming in it for most of her life. But after the scares she'd received today, she didn't mind one bit the way Bodie and his men were circling the wagons for her. Two times already, Bodie had saved her from a fate she'd experienced time and again in her nightmares.

She shifted on the bench to face him, knocking her knee against his. He didn't move his knee or his hand from the top of her thigh. He was making thinking difficult, but she made herself focus. "Thank you, again, Bodie. For saving me twice today. And for continuing to keep me safe. You don't have to, you know."

He finally lifted his hand from her leg to skim a strand of hair away from her face. His fingers lingered on her hair, his elbow propped on the top of the bench seat. "You saved yourself the first time. You executed quite the fake-out move on Kraken. I was very impressed."

His praise warmed her as much as his hand. "I got lucky, once. I doubt I could have done it twice. Fortunately, I didn't have to find out because you were there."

"Along with two other men."

"It was just you when Nightshade was charging at me. I wouldn't be sitting here if you hadn't yanked me up and out of the way."

"With my super strength, right?"

She laughed. "Yes." Him asking her what super power she'd pick seemed a lifetime ago. She grew serious again, turning her coffee cup on the specked Formica table top. "But now what?"

He pulled in a deep breath. "I should take you home, to the Wright Ranch. I doubt whoever this joker is would risk trying to hurt you there on the ranch."

Everything in her rebelled at the thought of giving up on her promise to her mom. "So you'd let him run me off?"

"If it means you'll be safe, then absolutely."

"But there is no guarantee I'll be safe there. As far as I know, my whole family is somewhere around here at the rodeo grounds. At least during the day. I saw everyone except Drew at one point or another today. And if this person does try something, I'm not sure anyone will be around to help me deal with him."

He pressed his lips together in obvious frustration, but his touch on her hair remained gentle. "Is someone staying with you in your trailer?"

"Alec was there icing his wrist when I left to look for you."

"He's hurt? He was hurt riding Bit O' Honey?" He sounded as if he was personally responsible for Alec's injury.

"I think it was more that Alec wasn't entirely prepared for the realities of bull riding."

Bodie released his breath. "Ah. Yeah, well, there's nothing easy about riding a bucking bull."

"Do you miss it?"

"Every damn day. There's no rush like it."

"That's what Alec said, that it was a rush."

"Until it's not, of course." His free hand drifted to his midsection.

She reached out and covered his hand with hers. He tried to move it away.

She resisted. "Bodie, it's okay."

He dropped his hand from her hair and his elbow from the back of the bench so he could take her hand into both of his. "No, Caitlin, it's—"

She leaned forward and cut him off with a kiss. If she couldn't convince him with words she wouldn't be repelled by him, then she'd show him.

He groaned and released her hand to bury both of his hands in her hair. She opened her mouth to him and he deepened the kiss, touching his tongue to hers. The contact sent a jolt of pleasure through her with a kick similar to being soaking wet and grabbing an electrified fence. She wanted more. She wanted all of him. She had to convince him there was nothing about him that could repel her.

With both her hands free now, she reached for the buttons on the front of his shirt and started unbuttoning them, working her way downward while he continued to rock her world with a simple kiss. She'd freed roughly half the buttons when he pulled back from her, capturing her hands in his.

"Caitlin—"

"Did I ever tell you about when Liam fell off the roof of the old barn and broke his leg? It was a compound fracture, so—"

"This—" he brought her hands lightly against his stomach "—is no broken leg."

"I know, Bodie. And neither was what happened to my mom. I know what a bull can do to flesh and bone."

"Then why would you ever want to be in the arena with one? Or here with me, a walking reminder?"

"Because I need to face my fears. I want the life I had before back. I want the person I was before back. Don't you?"

"No. I was an arrogant asshole."

She smiled and kissed him. It was supposed to be a quick kiss, a you-are-so-not-an-arrogant-asshole-any-more kiss, but the second her mouth connected with his, she was instantly lost. The man knew how to kiss.

It was her turn to groan. She arched toward him and his

hands released hers to slide around her waist and pull her closer.

The table was in the way.

"Ah, hell," he muttered and pulled away from her.

"Bodie—" she started to protest, but realized he was sliding from the dinette and reaching to pull her up with him. She scooted from the bench and rose to her feet. He didn't step back, so her breasts brushed against his chest. He settled his hands on her hips and brought her fully against him.

He was so hard and hot and handsome, she nearly melted into a puddle at his feet, but she was determined to address the elephant in the fifth wheel. To prove to him she wouldn't run shrieking from the RV. She leaned back far enough to see the remaining buttons on his long-sleeve, button-down shirt.

"Caitlin." His tone alone was enough to stop her, but his hands rose from her hips to capture hers again.

She met his storm-gray gaze, praying he could see the conviction in hers. "Bodie, I swear I won't be—"

"I had a girlfriend, you know."

She stilled. "No, I didn't."

"Elizabeth Howe. Not from around here. I met her when I was on the top national tour. I realize now she was just a big city version of your run-of-the-mill buckle bunny, but at the time…well, at the time I thought I was finally hitting it big both in the arena and out."

He paused and pulled in a deep breath, as if he'd never formed the words out loud before. "She was in the stands watching when Porky Chops left his permanent tattoo on me, and your cousin—" His voice hitched and caught, like the painful memory was a spiny burr forever lodged in his throat.

Caitlin swayed toward him, drawn by her need to comfort him. "Oh Bodie—"

"Anyway, she was there at the hospital, holding vigil at my bedside after I got out of surgery, until my dad and brothers showed up. They, of course, wanted to see…well, you know how ranch people are. They weren't going to be satisfied until they saw for themselves if the docs had closed me up well enough."

Caitlin wanted so badly to wrap her arms around him and stop what she feared she knew was coming. Instead, she let him speak.

He pulled in another shuddering breath. "Needless to say, the minute she saw what was under the bandages, and I assured my family my bull riding days were over, she was out of there like a shot. I never saw her again."

"I'm not her, Bodie."

"I know. And I also know it would hurt more to lose you."

Caitlin pulled her hands from his and reached up to cup his face. "You won't lose me. I'm ranch people, too, Bodie. You know I am. Please, trust me."

He closed his eyes for a moment, as if fighting a war with himself, then he leaned down and captured her mouth with his. She could taste his surrender, and her heart sang.

She dropped her hands from his face, and he guided them to the remaining fastened buttons on his shirt. She concentrated solely on freeing the buttons from their holes before she broke away from his kiss and allowed herself to look at the aftermath of a bull putting a hole in him. When the last button was released, she pushed his shirt aside to reveal his broad, muscled, and yes, scarred, chest and stomach with a light dusting of short dark hair over his well-defined pecs. She'd been expecting one long, maybe jagged, welted scar much like Josh's elbow, but instead Bodie had several scars radiating out from a slightly puckered center of scar tissue about the size of a half-dollar. The bull's horn must have torn him, as well as impaled him. It was nothing short of a miracle that he was alive.

She looked up into his stormy gray eyes watching her intently and told him the truth. "I was expecting worse."

He released his breath in a bark of laughter. "Is that so?"

"As matter of fact, yes." She placed the tip of her index finger on the center mass of scar tissue. "Is it sensitive?"

The ridges of his still well-defined stomach muscles quivered. "Not really. The edges of the smaller ones are sometimes."

Trying to keep her touch feather-light, Caitlin traced the bottom-most scar toward his waistband. "My very own North Star to follow."

His stomach muscles convulsed.

When she dipped her finger down below the waistband of his low-slung jeans, he grabbed her hand. "Okay, enough show and tell."

"But aren't you going to show me your *big buckles*?"

He searched her face, her eyes.

She didn't blink. She wanted this with him. Needed it. Needed him.

"Do you want to see my big buckles?"

She rocked toward him, drawn to him as she had been when he was atop his big gelding and she'd been dressed as a clown. Then, their attraction had been purely physical. And free of complication because they hadn't known each other's identity. But now, even knowing all the reasons they shouldn't be together, she wanted him more. Because she believed she was coming to know who he really was.

She slid her free hand around his waist beneath his shirt, savoring his smooth soft skin. "Yes, Bodie. Very much."

She thought he was going to kiss her again, but instead he turned and started leading her toward the short steps to his bedroom. He stopped first at the trailer door and turned the small lock on the door.

"Wait, you're going to lock Danny and Cabe out?"

He raised an eyebrow at her. "You want them to come in?"

"Well, no, not while…you know…while we're…you know," she sputtered.

He continued to the bedroom. "I actually wasn't thinking of them," he said, his tone serious.

She balked. "Oh. Do you think…?"

"I don't intend to find out."

Caitlin stared at the door, wondering if the man with the cattle prod could be bold enough to come after her—or Bodie—inside his fifth wheel.

Bodie stepped in front of her, capturing her attention.

He put a hand to the side of her face and skimmed her cheek with his thumb. "I won't let anyone hurt you, Caitlin. I swear it. You can trust me."

She believed him. "I know. I do." She went up on her toes and kissed him. He kissed her back like a man too long without what he really needed. Her hands immediately sought his bare skin, pushing aside his shirt so she could skim her palms over his sides, his hard pecs, his stomach.

He flinched.

She stopped her roaming, but didn't remove her hands. "Am I hurting you?"

He settled his forehead against hers. "No."

Her heart ached for what he'd been through, for what he was still putting himself through. "I won't hurt you, Bodie. I swear it. You can trust me," she echoed his words back at him.

He cupped her face with both of his hands. "I know. I do."

His trust in her made her heart sing. She took his hands from her face and lowered them to his side. Then she slid her hands up over his chest, her fingers grazing his pebbled nipples, then up to his strong, muscle-capped shoulders beneath his shirt. She pushed the shirt off him as she ran her touch down the back of his arms.

He let the shirt drop to the floor.

She leaned forward and kissed the indentation between his collar bones, his pecs, breathing in the incredible masculine, faintly spicy scent of him. She could feel his heart galloping in his chest. The knowledge she was responsible for his accelerated heart rate was empowering. Humbling.

He skimmed his hands up her arms and kissed her hair, then took her hand again and led her up the two short stairs to his bedroom. His back was a sculpted study in male perfection. She noticed he had a tan line at his arms and neck that she hadn't noticed while facing him. His scar, while not in the least bit repellant to her, had nonetheless commanded her attention. He obviously rarely took his shirt off these days. The physical proof of how self-conscious he was of his scar tore at her. She wanted so badly to make him at ease about what he'd been through. At least with her.

Though it had been mere hours, it felt like a lifetime ago since she'd been in here with Bodie, seen him struggling with his demons from the past. Demons she'd stirred. Would he stop what was happening between them again?

She dearly hoped not.

After sliding the pocket door shut and turning the latch to lock it, he led her to the bed, which consumed most of the space. The sole light on was a small reading lamp mounted on the wall above the headboard, so when he turned back toward her, his face was shadowed. She couldn't tell if he was happy or resigned, so she opened her mouth to ask if he was okay, if what they were about to do—if they were really about to do it—was really okay with him.

He stopped her from speaking with a kiss. A long, deep, passionate kiss that melted her into him. She put her arms around his neck to anchor herself to him.

He certainly seemed okay with what they were doing.

And when he slipped his hands behind her and grasped

her bottom, bringing her hips flush against his, any doubts she had left her brain right along with the ability to form rational thought.

He broke off the kiss and looked down at her with a grin. "That good, eh?"

It was only then that she realized she'd moaned. "Actually, yes. Do it again. Please."

He chuckled. "Yes, ma'am." He dipped his head to capture her mouth again, but this time teasing at her lips with his tongue, his teeth. He released her bottom and brought his hands up her sides to her breasts.

He hummed in appreciation, then set his fingers to work on the buttons of her shirt. "You have too many clothes on. I want this off."

She leaned back to give him better access, pulling the elastic band holding her hair off and tucking it into her back pocket. She thought about making good use of this time to unfasten his belt and jeans, but the brush of his hands on her breasts as he worked his way down the buttons of her shirt completely distracted her. She wasn't inexperienced, but nothing—or no one—could prepare her for the reality of a man like Bodie Hadley.

So she stood as motionless as she could while his fortunately clever fingers made quick work of unbuttoning her shirt. Too late she remembered she still wore the sports bra she'd donned beneath the bullfighting gear. Frilly lingerie it was not.

She had to fight not to giggle. "Just wait until you get to the shin guards."

His dark brows went up. "You're still wearing them?"

"I've been a little distracted today."

He bent to kiss her neck. "Hmm. You and me both."

He worked his way down to her collarbone then straightened to slip her shirt from her shoulders and arms. He tossed her shirt toward the end of the bed, then considered her sports bra as if it were a complicated piece of tack. She took pity on him and quickly unfastened the hidden hook and eye closures on the front of the bra.

He grinned. "Ah."

Suddenly self-conscious herself, she hesitated, holding the halves of the bra together.

"Caitlin," he drew her gaze to his. "You are beautiful. Absolutely, stunningly beautiful. And I can't believe you are here, with me." His hand drifted to his scar.

Empathy for him engulfed her, and she forgot about her silly insecurities and wrapped her arms around him. Bodie's arms went around her and they simply held each other tight. But slowly awareness crept in, and Caitlin realized her sports bra had opened again and her bare breasts were now pressed firmly against the hot skin of his chest. He seemed to notice the same thing because his breathing changed, and his body stirred against her.

Then he was kissing her. Urgently. Passionately.

Caitlin's brain emptied of everything except for her need to be as close to Bodie as she humanly could. She wasn't sure who removed what, but the next thing she knew, she was bare, save the red socks and shin guards beneath.

Bodie paused in the act of shucking his jeans and briefs

at the same time. He grinned at her. "I say leave them on."

"For protection?"

He snorted a laugh, then paused. "Hang on a sec." He pulled his britches back up and started to slip past her, but paused to kiss her, first her mouth, then her breast.

Her knees went weak.

He pulled away and gestured at the bed. "Climb in. I'll be right back."

Figuring he was going to find the proper sort of protection, she pulled the thick comforter and sheet back on the bed and dove beneath them. Then she set to work on removing the knee-high sport socks and the shin guards under them. While the notion of leaving them on had been funny, no way was she actually going to do it.

She could hear Bodie opening the small vanity in the miniscule bathroom and unzipping what was probably his shaving kit. She heard him say, "Oh, thank God," before he flicked off the bathroom light and reemerged. Sure enough, he held what looked to be more than one square foil packet.

The relief on his face made her heart race. "We're good. I wasn't sure there, for a second, but we're set." He went to the other side of the bed and dropped his pants, removing everything in one motion. Guys had such amazing, peculiar talents.

This guy in particular was amazing to look at too. Caitlin's mouth went dry and her heart began to race.

He slid into the bed next to her and gathered her close to him. But instead of getting busy, as she expected, he brushed her hair back from her face and simply looked at her.

He placed the tip of one finger beneath her left eye. "Why the blue tear?"

"What?"

"When you were dressed as a clown for the parade, you'd painted a blue tear right here." He caressed the spot again.

"Oh, that," she tried to sound flippant about it, like it was nothing, but the steel of his gray eyes made it clear he wasn't buying it. She ran her finger down the crease between his pecs as she tried to come up with something plausible. "Most clowns are sad, right?"

"Not really, no."

She shrugged. "Then I guess I'm about as good at being a clown as I am at being a bullfighter."

Bodie shifted part of his weight onto her and held her face between his hands, clearly wanting her to pay attention. "Caitlin, you are wonderful. You can do anything you set your mind to. You've already shown me that in the short time I've known you." He lowered his head and kissed the spot where she'd painted the tear. "I don't want you to be a sad clown. Not ever again."

Then he made love to her, slowly and sure. Expertly, with tender care, leaving no doubt he desired her.

And she knew she would never be the same again.

CHAPTER FOURTEEN

C AITLIN WOKE THE next morning the same way she'd fallen asleep, wrapped in Bodie's warm embrace.

Bodie Hadley, of all people.

She was going to have to figure out a way to make her relationship with him acceptable to her family. How, she had no idea. But she needed to. A warmth she'd never experienced before filled her chest as she lay in his bed, in his arms. She nuzzled against the back of the hand that he'd tucked beneath her cheek as he slept. She wanted him in her life.

He deserved a second chance.

His breathing changed, and he stirred behind her. In all sorts of ways.

She smiled and squirmed against him.

He hummed and tightened his arms around her, drawing her closer against him. "Mornin', sunshine," he murmured into her hair.

"Good morning."

"It definitely is a good morning." He slipped his hand from beneath her cheek and roamed it over her bare skin. The delicious rasp of his calluses raised goosebumps all over her.

As much as she'd have loved to stay right where she was forever, she couldn't help but begin to worry about what the day would hold. "What are you going to do today?"

"Besides you?" He raised his head and kissed her ear.

The warmth in her chest expanded until she thought she might burst from it. "*After* that."

"I'll worry about it in, oh, five minutes."

"Five?" she laughed.

"You are very delectable in the morning, and I'm a morning kinda guy." He slid a muscled leg over hers, shifted her onto her back, and moved atop her.

She smiled and threaded her fingers into his thick, tousled black hair.

Someone banged on the fifth wheel's door.

Caitlin's entire body jerked in surprise and fear.

Bodie heaved a chest-expanding sigh and dropped his head to her shoulder. "I really need to buy a *Do Not Disturb* sign."

"What if it's one of my brothers? Even Alec will freak if he finds me here—"

He raised his head and propped his weight on his elbows. "Not to worry, it isn't one of your brothers. It's one of my guys."

"How do you know?"

"I heard whoever it is try the handle first. I've learned from experience your brothers strictly bang." Stroking her hair from her face in a way she had come to love, he said, "To be continued later. Okay?"

She smiled up at him. "Yes, please."

He smiled back with unmistakable tenderness before dropping a kiss on the end of her nose. He hoisted himself off her with a flex of biceps that had her dragging her hands along his arms as he left the bed. He was nothing short of gorgeous.

She instantly missed Bodie's heat. Pulling the sheet up to cover herself, she watched him don his briefs and jeans in the same way he'd removed them, in one smooth motion. He dug out a clean shirt from a built-in dresser and pulled it on, buttoning it enough to cover his scar.

Catching her watching him, he put his hands and a knee on the bed and leaned in to capture her mouth in a toe-curling kiss. Additional banging made him break off the kiss she wished would never end.

"Damn," Bodie grumbled as he pushed himself from the bed and headed for the pocket door. "If I didn't know better, I'd think the universe was conspiring to keep us apart." He winked at her while he unlocked the pocket door and slid it open.

No, but our families certainly will. The thought blazed through her brain as she watched him slide the pocket door closed behind him. Knowing she shouldn't be caught here in Bodie's bed by anyone, but realizing she didn't actually care, she scooted to the side of the bed where most of her clothes were piled on the floor. At first she couldn't find her shirt, until she remembered Bodie had tossed it to the other side of the bed, much the same way he'd flung the protective vest he'd slipped off her the first time they'd kissed.

Right before he'd stopped what they were doing. But he

hadn't stopped them last night.

And she'd never been happier about anything in her life.

BODIE PICKED UP the shirt Caitlin had peeled off him last night with a smile he couldn't seem to wipe off his face before he unlocked the fifth wheel's door and swung it open.

Danny stood on the other side looking like he hadn't slept the night before. Probably similar to how Bodie looked, minus the grin.

"Why don't I smell coffee?" Danny groused as he climbed the steps into the trailer. "I need coffee." He shook the thermos in his hand as if to prove the point it was empty.

Bodie glanced at the pocket door to make sure he'd closed it all the way behind him when he'd left the bedroom. "I haven't made any yet." Hopefully Danny wouldn't want to wait for it to brew and would go looking for his morning shot of caffeine somewhere else.

Bodie needed Danny gone long enough for Caitlin to slip out. While Bodie didn't care if the whole world knew who he'd had in his bed last night, Caitlin might not be ready for anyone to know. Yet. Though he should, he had no intention of sneaking around with her. She was a woman to be proud of. Even if she was a Neisson.

But before he kicked Danny out, Bodie wanted to find out how the night went for him. "Anything happen with the bulls last night?"

Danny plopped down at the dinette. "Nope. I pulled the

dually close enough to have a good view of our pens without being obvious I was there to watch them. Cabe came to spell me around two, but instead of leaving, I just crashed out right there in the truck."

Bodie took pity on him and started the coffee, dumping extra scoops in to make the brew even stronger than he normally made it. Which was strong, even for cowboy coffee. He'd need some, also, to stay awake after the rather active night he and Caitlin had shared. "Is Cabe still there?"

"Snoring away. He woke me around four-thirty or five because he couldn't stay awake any longer. But I need coffee if I'm going to be of any use today. There are enough people we know walking around now that I figured the bulls would be fine." Danny took off his hat and set it on the table to scrub at his hair. "I also wanted to check on you." He eyed Bodie, from his bed-head hair to his half-buttoned shirt to his wrinkled jeans and bare feet. "Do you know if Caitlin is okay?"

"She's fine," was all Bodie was willing to say.

The pocket door slid open. "Morning, Danny," Caitlin said from the bedroom doorway. She was fully dressed and her hair was back in a sleek ponytail.

Danny blinked at her and at Bodie, then grinned. "Well, good morning, Caitlin."

Huh. Well, apparently she didn't mind if their newly minted relationship was out in the open. A warm swell of what could only be satisfaction spread through Bodie.

She closed her eyes and pulled in a deep breath. "Ahh, thank you, Jesus. Coffee." It had barely started to brew, but the heavenly aroma was already filling the trailer. She came down the steps and sat across from Danny at the table. "Did I hear you say that nothing happened with the bulls last night?"

Still grinning like an idiot, Danny answered, "Yes, ma'am."

She pulled in a breath. "That's good for you all, but maybe not so good for me."

Bodie stepped toward her and ran what he hoped to be a comforting hand over her shoulder. "We'll figure out what's going on, Cait. I promise."

Danny nodded his agreement, though the look of near-glee on his face led Bodie to believe he was thinking of something other than catching the cattle prod wielder. He also didn't seem to mind one bit that Bodie had been knocking boots with a Neisson. At least not the pretty one.

"Well," Danny said, pushing himself out of the dinette bench. "I had better get my coffee and leave you two...to it." He waved vaguely in their direction, not even trying to conceal his amusement. "Don't worry about a thing. Cabe and I will see to the bulls."

Bodie's hand drifted of its own accord to the satin skin on the back of Caitlin's neck. "I'd planned on fastening Boomerang's trough to the pen railing—"

Danny shook his head as he poured some of the coffee that had finished brewing into his thermos. "Don't you worry about that. I'll handle it."

Ever grateful that his men's dedication to his bulls rivaled his own, Bodie said, "Thank you, Danny. I appreciate everything you and Cabe are doing to help me out here."

Danny screwed the thermos lid on, picked up his hat from the table and returned it to his head, then slapped Bodie on the back on his way to the door. "It's just good to have you back, boss."

Caitlin's hand slipped around the back of his thigh and squeezed as Danny shut the door behind him with a soft *click*. "Ian says you can judge a man by how much his horse likes him. But I think you can judge a man by how much the people close to him like him." She looked up at him, her blue eyes bright. "You're a good man, Bodie Hadley."

His throat closed tight. He'd grown so used to being the bad guy, that her words, and the obvious sentiment behind them, were almost too much for him to bear. He leaned down and dropped what he intended to be a quick kiss on her soft lips. But there was no such thing as a quick kiss for him where Caitlin was concerned, so he kissed her good and long. He almost pulled her up and hauled her back to bed, but reality had indeed intruded. He needed to get her safe.

He broke off the kiss and stepped away from her. Clearing his throat, he said, "Let's get you that coffee."

Her cheeks flushed, she smiled at him. "That would be great."

He pulled a clean mug for her from the cupboard. "Not gonna lie, you surprised me when you opened that door." He nodded toward the pocket door as he poured her coffee. "I was all set to blame any noise you might have made on mice."

She paled. "Do you have mice in here?"

"No," he laughed.

"Good." But she shuddered a little anyway. "I hope you're okay with me outing us."

"I am." He handed her the full mug, plus the creamer and sugar for her to doctor her coffee as she pleased. "So you'll be okay with me taking you back to your family, to the Wright Ranch if necessary, and filling them in on what's going on?" No way was he letting her out of his sight until he knew she had a cavalry surrounding her.

She paused for a moment while adding creamer to her coffee. "I am," she echoed his words back to him.

"Facing your fears, and all that?"

"I'm not afraid of my family, Bodie."

He snorted into his coffee cup. "That makes one of us." He was afraid of not only her family, but the rift her being with him would cause. Maybe he should be more worried about protecting her, not only from the bulls and the guy setting them on her, but from himself too.

AFTER FORTIFYING THEMSELVES with as much coffee as they dared and Bodie giving himself a quick spit-polish, they left his fifth wheel for her family's trailer. Hopefully someone would be around to alert about what had transpired with Nightshade the evening before.

Caitlin had a hard time not slipping her hand into Bodie's or threading her arm through his as they walked the short distance together. But they were drawing enough stares from those they passed just by walking together. Hadley and Neisson. She wanted to tell them to get over it.

Bodie staring down every man who came within twelve feet of her didn't help.

She bumped shoulders with him. "Stop glowering at everyone."

"I'm not glowering. But any one of these guys could be the one trying to hurt you."

"No," she dismissed the notion, but she did start looking at the men a little differently. Especially the ones roughly Bodie's height and build. She really had thought she'd been following him last night.

By the time they reached her trailer, her nerves were stretched tight. Hopefully no one would be in the trailer so she'd have a chance to clean up and change before she had to face any of her brothers.

Bodie stepped forward and opened the trailer door for her. She stepped inside and came to a sudden stop. Ian was seated at the dinette table across from a man Caitlin didn't know, with two white binders open to what looked to be breeder's spreadsheets on the table between them. There was something about the man that niggled at her.

She guessed him to be in his mid-forties, but with his olive-green baseball cap pulled low, his heavy beard and sun-weathered skin, she couldn't be sure. Something about him was definitely familiar, though. Then she realized he'd been the one glaring at her before the parade. Before she could ask him about it, the man muttered something to Ian about having to leave, closed the binders, and gathered them to his chest. He hurriedly slid from the seat and stood.

But Ian's focus was solely on her. He frowned. "Caitlin, where—?"

Bodie's hand at her back, urging her forward into the trailer so he could enter behind her, stopped Ian mid-question.

The man Ian had been meeting with, probably a vendor pitching a new bloodline to introduce to the Wright's prize-winning American Bucking Bulls, hurried past her and Bodie and left the trailer without a word.

Caitlin pointed at the door, which the guy had left open, and asked Ian, "Who was that?"

Ian ignored her question and stood, his now glowering attention solely on Bodie.

Bodie flexed his fingers on the small of her back, a gesture she took to mean reassurance, before moving away from her.

Ian planted his fists on his hips. "Hadley, you better tell me you are simply returning my little sister to where she belongs after telling her *no*." He was obviously referring to the warning he'd delivered to Bodie when Ian had been looking for her after the sponsors' party.

Annoyance flared hot in Caitlin. "Ian—"

Her brother raised a hand to stop her. "I'll deal with you later." He shifted his flinty blue gaze back to Bodie. "You promised me—"

"Your sister is in danger," Bodie stated succinctly.

"She's...what?"

Bodie said, "You know about the near miss with Kraken,

right?"

"Which wouldn't have happened if you—"

Having had enough of her brother's condemnation of Bodie, Caitlin interjected, "It happened again, Ian. Well, sort of. Last night, I was trying to catch up with—" she stopped herself, not wanting to throw fuel on his anti-Bodie fire by admitting she'd thought she'd been chasing after Bodie, instead saying, "someone, and I saw him go into a funnel chute. And I followed. But once I was inside, whoever it was that I had been following—not my friend, obviously—closed the gate behind me, then opened the other gate and used a cattle prod on the bull that was in the holding pen."

Ian's eyes narrowed.

Bodie said, "It was Nightshade. He prodded Nightshade into charging her inside a funnel chute."

Ian's hands dropped from his hips, and he took a step toward her. He knew better than anyone how the incident with their mother and grandfather's bull had affected her.

She rushed to reassure him, despite being annoyed with him, "I'm okay. But only because Bodie had seen me and followed me to make sure I was okay. He lifted me out of the chute before Nightshade could destroy me."

Ian shifted his attention to Bodie. "Did you see him? Did you see who tried to hurt her?"

"If I had, I wouldn't be here talking to you. I'd be hurting him worse."

Caitlin believed him.

Obviously Ian did, too, because he gave Bodie a nod of approval. Then he strode to Caitlin and gathered her into a crushing hug. "I'm so sorry, peanut."

He sounded as though he was at fault. And not just for erroneously blaming Bodie.

She needed to know why. "Ian—"

"What the hell is this?" A deep, gruff voice asked from the doorway.

Grandfather.

Ian released her, and they both turned to find their grandfather standing in the open trailer doorway looking at Bodie as if he was a huge, fresh, steaming pile of bull shit somehow deposited in their trailer.

Their father appeared behind him, peering past his father at them. When he noticed Bodie, his eyebrows shot up to his receding hairline. "Ian, Caitlin? What is—?"

Grandfather stepped to the side and growled, "Get the hell out of my trailer, Hadley."

Bodie's body went stiff and his expression shuddered. He looked to Ian. "Keep her safe."

Without meeting her gaze or so much as glancing at her, he walked through the opening her grandfather had made for him.

"Bodie!" Caitlin called and started after him, but Ian snagged her arm and held her at his side.

Her grandfather and dad entered the trailer, closing the door behind them.

Caitlin yanked her arm from her brother's grip. "He saved my life. Twice!"

Her father said, "He was responsible for your cousin's death, Caitlin."

Her jaw dropped and her gasp of disbelief caught in her throat. "How can you say that? It was an accident. An awful, regrettable accident that happened when he and Charlie were both doing their jobs. You know that!"

Grandfather moved to sit on the couch at the front of the trailer. "He's a Hadley, Caitlin," he pronounced, as if being a Hadley was synonymous with mass genocide.

Caitlin rushed to sit next to the man she used to follow around like his shadow. "But what does that mean? Why do you hate them so much?" She looked to her father, and he simply shrugged like hating the Hadleys was simply a part of life. Like losing the ones you loved.

She slipped a hand beneath her grandfather's big, sun- and age-weathered hand. "Please tell me why."

He curled his strong fingers around her hand. He pulled in a breath that expanded his barrel chest, then released it with a sigh. "That boy's grandfather stole the love of my life."

Caitlin pulled back her chin. She looked to her father and Ian, but they were both blinking at Thomas Wright with the same expressions of shock and confusion she was certain she wore.

Her dad said, "You mean Mom?"

Her grandfather scoffed. "No, not your mother. I met her later." He held up his free hand. "And don't get me wrong, I loved her. Hell, I still love her." He heaved another sigh. "No, I'm talking about my first love. Bill Hadley stole away Rebecca Jameson, married her, and got her pregnant before I could win her back."

Caitlin shook her head, struggling to grasp what her grandfather, a man she'd always thought of as rational and infinitely practical, was saying. "You mean you've hated and vilified an entire family because your old girlfriend picked someone else?"

"She didn't—"

Caitlin couldn't bear it. "I'm sorry, Grandfather, but yeah, she did." Caitlin thought of the way Bodie made her feel, despite what she knew she should feel toward him. "And she probably couldn't help it."

Caitlin looked to Ian for backup, but he just rolled his eyes and nodded as if to say *keep going, peanut. You got this.*

She covered her grandfather's hand with her other hand. "Grandfather, you ended up with a wonderful woman who helped you build an amazing, successful life, with a family who loves you. Don't you think it's time to let it go?"

He slanted her a look with those icy blue eyes of his, and she swallowed hard. She might have gone too far.

He grumbled, "If we're getting over the past, I'll expect you in the bull barn next week, Caitlin Ann." He slid his hand from hers, rose from the couch, and left the trailer with a slam of the door.

Caitlin looked between her father and Ian.

Her dad shrugged as if to say *you heard the man.*

Ian's grin said *now you've stepped in it, peanut.*

But all she could think was *does Bodie know?*

He deserved to know. She had to tell him that the hatred her family, and those connected to them, had been taught to feel toward his family had nothing to do with him. He was not the villain in any of this. He never had been.

Her father moved to the couch and took Grandfather's vacated seat. He gathered her hand into his as she'd done to her grandfather. "Since we're also explaining motivations, I'd like you to tell me why you've decided to overcome what's happened to you by becoming a bullfighter, of all things, and why now?"

With both her father and oldest brother staring at her, Caitlin couldn't think of a solid excuse other than the truth, so she decided to just tell them. "I promised Mom, right before she died, that I would keep Alec safe. He'd just told her he intended to become a bull rider."

She felt her father's shock and surprise in his grip on her hand, so she rushed to add, "I couldn't talk him out of it, even though I've been trying for months, and the only other way I could think to fulfill my promise was to be in the arena when Alec rode."

Ian said, "Caitlin, Mom was pretty out of it at the end. She made me promise to keep the wood elves from beating up the barn fairies."

Stunned, Caitlin could only stare at Ian.

Her father squeezed her hand. "She made me promise to take that trip around the world I'd always dreamed of, on my motorcycle."

Caitlin blinked at her dad. "But you've never had a motorcycle, have you?"

He smiled sadly. "No, I have never had a motorcycle. Nor have I ever talked of wanting one, because I never have. I've also never wanted to travel around the world. As Ian said, your mother was not exactly herself at the end."

Caitlin sat back, not sure what to make of this revelation. If her mother had been making outlandish requests of her family, Caitlin probably wasn't obligated to keep the promise she'd made to her. Or was she? She wasn't sure.

One thing she was sure of was how good putting on J.D.'s jersey had felt.

She needed to talk to Bodie about this, as well.

Caitlin dropped a quick kiss on her father's cheek and rose from the couch. "I'll be right back, Dad."

"Cait—" Ian called to her as she headed out the door.

She called back over her shoulder, "I'll be fine, Ian. There're too many people around for anyone to try something." Bodie couldn't have gone far. She had to find him and tell him what she'd learned.

She hurried toward the bull pens, figuring that was the most likely place for Bodie to have gone after he left her family's trailer. She wove her way through the other RVs and stock trailers, keeping her eyes open for Bodie. When she reached the space between the second to the last row of trailers, she heard a vehicle behind her. She glanced over her shoulder and saw a white, late model pickup truck being driven between the trailers. She moved to the side to allow the truck to pass, but it stopped right next to her.

The man Ian had been meeting with in her family's trailer hopped out and moved with purpose toward her. A man roughly Bodie's height and build.

A shiver stampeded down her spine.

She turned to run, but her ankle twisted and she stumbled. He grabbed her, his grip hard on her biceps. "You're coming with me, brat. Get in the truck."

"No! Let go of me!" Caitlin struggled to free herself from his hold, but the pain in her ankle and his tight grip impeded her.

And with a blaze of terror, Caitlin realized where she knew him from.

He was the one her mother had been angry with in the vault in her grandfather's bull barn.

CHAPTER FIFTEEN

B ODIE CHECKED THE fasteners the guys had used to secure Boomerang's trough to the metal bar of his pen. He stepped back and watched the big bull nose the trough in an attempt to flip it again. But Boomerang couldn't, because Danny and Cabe had done an excellent job. Bodie could count on them.

Just as he could count on the Wrights and Neissons hating the Hadleys.

The gloom he'd felt since leaving—hell, who was he kidding, he'd *run* from—the Hadleys' trailer nearly overwhelmed him. He propped his forearms on the top rail of Boomerang's pen to help support his weight.

He should have stayed.

Then he'd know for sure Caitlin was safe.

He'd promised her he'd keep her safe, but all it took was the stink eye from Old Man Wright and Bodie had run for the hills. Caitlin wouldn't think he was a good man now.

Why hadn't he stayed and proven to her she could count on him?

And why did he think it was too late? His heart was still beating in his scarred-up chest. He was still breathing, wasn't he? The only thing stopping him was his own cowardice, his idiocy. He could still prove to her he could be taught.

That he was worthy of her.

He realized with a flash of clarity that he wanted to be worthy of her, because he wanted her in his life. He'd fallen for her.

Hard.

If he had to prove to her family every damn day for the rest of his sorry life that he was worthy of her, he would do just that.

Starting right now.

Bodie straightened and pushed off from Boomerang's pen. Readjusting his cowboy hat on his head, he headed off for Caitlin's family's trailer with a purposeful stride. He'd just passed the first row of stock trailers when he heard a man's raised voice.

"Get in the damn truck, you little bitch."

"Go to hell! Help! Help me!"

Caitlin.

A cold sluice of fear hit him that was one hundred times worse than what he'd felt when Kraken and Nightshade had nearly reached her. He knew exactly what a bull could do. They were a known threat. But at this moment, he had no idea what danger Caitlin faced or from whom.

He exploded into a run and rounded the corner of the next row of trailers. A white truck was parked between the rows, with the driver's door open, and a man trying to shove Caitlin into the cab. She'd planted one booted foot on the door frame with the other held up off the ground and was clinging to the edge of the open door with both hands, making it impossible for the guy to shove her in.

Bodie recognized her attacker. He was the man who'd been sitting across the dinette table from Ian Neisson in their trailer. But now it appeared he was trying to kidnap Caitlin.

Over Bodie's dead body.

Bodie ran full speed at them.

The guy must have heard Bodie coming because he released Caitlin and turned toward him.

Which made it easier for Bodie to tackle him, putting the full force of his weight and momentum into the hit. The guy's baseball cap and Bodie's cowboy hat flew off. Bodie was considerably bigger, and infinitely angrier, so he wasn't surprised to hear the crack of ribs and the guy's breath leaving him with a whoosh and a strangled gasp of pain.

Using his knee in the man's sternum to hold him down, Bodie reared up with a clenched fist cocked and ready to pound the guy's face in if he resisted.

Bodie really, really wanted him to resist.

But the man beneath him had his hands up to ward off any blows, not to fight. For half a second, Bodie considered destroying the guy with his fists anyway.

"Bodie. Bodie, you got him. It's okay. I'm okay. You got him," Caitlin coaxed him down from his rage.

He looked up to see her standing next them, her weight on only one foot and her hands out like she was trying to settle a spooked horse. And that's exactly how he felt, spooked he might lose her.

Not worrying if he caused additional injury, Bodie

shoved off from the man he'd tackled and went to Caitlin.

Cupping her head between his hands, he searched her flushed face for any sign she'd been harmed in any way. "Are you hurt anywhere? Did he hurt you?"

She held him at the waist, gripping his shirt. "No. I'm fine. Well, I twisted my ankle, but I'm good. You saved me. Again." She gave him a trembling smile.

Fine my ass. She'd been scared to death.

He released her and turned back toward the man to finish what he'd started.

Caitlin tugged at his arm. "No, Bodie. It's okay. He's not going anywhere."

Other people had heard the commotion and were hurrying toward them. His oldest brother, Garrett, and Liam amongst them. Garrett reached them first.

Bodie pointed at the man clutching his ribs on the ground. "He attacked her, Garrett. Call the cops."

Garrett looked between Bodie, Caitlin, and the guy on the ground. "What the hell, Bodie?"

"I'll tell you all about it later. Just get the cops."

For once, his brother didn't argue with him and pulled his phone from his pocket.

Caitlin tugged on him again. "I know who he is, Bodie. I realized who he was right as he was grabbing me. I remember now."

That caught Bodie's full attention.

"He worked for a short time at my grandfather's ranch ten years ago. He had more hair on the top of his head and none on his face then. He was who my mom was angry with that day in the vault. I only had a glimpse of him before Mom pulled me back out, but now I remember seeing him. I guess after watching Blackjack—" she stopped, her throat working. The trauma she'd suffered that day was plain on her face.

Bodie felt her pain as if it were his own. He gathered her in his arms. "Shh. I got you, Caitlin."

She pulled in a shuddering breath, then returned her attention to the man Bodie very much wanted to end at the moment.

Old Red and Liam had helped the man to a seated position.

Old Red pulled back. "Fletch? Is that you?"

Her grandfather's former ranch hand spit into the dirt then said, "Long time no see, Red."

Liam grabbed the man's bearded chin and turned his face to scrutinized him. "Karl Fletcher?"

Fletcher jerked away. "Get off me, Neisson."

Liam held tight to Fletcher's arm. "What the—"

Fletcher snarled, "I was afraid she would eventually remember. I couldn't risk her identifying me."

"For what?" Bodie asked.

Caitlin said, "I remember seeing him standing in front of an open cryo vat with a fistful of straws and a cooler at his feet."

Bodie looked between her and the ranch hand. "You were stealing bull sperm?"

Fletcher's face contorted in anger. "Stealing her granddaddy's *prized bull* sperm, that's what. I took care of the mom when I let that bull out. If I wanted any life at all, I had to get rid of this one too. Especially with her hanging around the rodeo now, where I'm trying to earn my living."

"A living selling stolen prized rough stock and bull sperm," Ian pronounced as he came up behind them.

Liam and Red jerked Fletcher to his feet. He howled.

Caitlin stepped away from Bodie and asked her brother, "Is that what you're invol—"

Ian stopped her with a look. "Of course not."

"But Ian—" Caitlin persisted.

"I'm not at liberty to discuss that right now, Caitlin."

Bodie knew the local rodeo association had been looking into a recent spat of bull straw thefts. Was Ian working with them?

Ian gestured toward the thief and said, "I didn't realize he was the new hire who'd disappeared the day mom was hurt. I'd been away at college." The self-recrimination was thick in his tone.

Bodie said, "It was a long time ago."

"Seems like yesterday," Ian said. "We didn't realize anything had been stolen because Grandfather destroyed all of Blackjack's straws."

Ian had left out the fact that Old Man Wright had also euthanized Blackjack, but the knowledge of what grief had done to Caitlin's grandfather hung heavy in the air.

Bodie retrieved his cowboy hat and dusted it off. He purposefully stepped on Karl Fletcher's cap.

"Hey!" Fletcher protested and glowered at Bodie. "I wish you'd died, too, the day I got rid of that other Neisson," he sneered.

Liam shook him and said, "What? Are you talking about Charlie?"

Fletcher glared at him. "He recognized me at the event where this idiot"—he pointed at Bodie—"was gored. He told me he wanted to talk to me after he was done bull-fighting. I figured I was busted, so I made sure as many bulls as possible were good and riled up, just like I did Kraken and Nightshade, before I took off again."

Bodie was rocked back on his heels by the revelation. While he remained on the hook for stupidly celebrating his successful ride on Porky Chop, even though he knew of the bull's well-known bad attitude, Charlie's death hadn't been all his fault after all. Learning the bull's nastiness had been heightened that day by a cattle prod, before Bodie had even climbed on him, was enough to buckle his knees.

Red said, "You were always a little off, Fletch, but you've completely lost your mind."

The bastard continued digging his own hole, "My life was ruined the day I had to run from the Wright Ranch. I couldn't sell what I'd taken, thousands of dollars worth of bull straws, because Wright put down that damn bull of his. Until Wright's daughter finally kicked it, I was always looking over my shoulder. I thought I was safe to come back home, but then I spotted her here." He nodded at Caitlin. "I couldn't risk her remembering what she'd seen before I set that bull loose on her and her mom."

"You son of a bitch," Caitlin swore.

Ian started toward him with his fists clenched, but two

police officers who'd been working security for the rodeo came jogging toward them. Bodie placed a staying hand on Ian's shoulder, despite how much he would love to see the bigger Neisson beat the guy to a pulp. This man needed to pay in a more permanent way.

A couple guys from sports medicine showed up with their first aid kit.

One of them said, "Who's hurt? We heard there was a fight."

The Fletcher said, "I am. I'm hurt."

Bodie rolled his eyes. "Not enough."

"Amen," Ian concurred.

Bodie looked to Caitlin, still not putting her weight on one foot. "And she is too."

She shook her head. "I just twisted my ankle, is all."

Ian said, "Let them look at it, Cait."

"Fine," she huffed, and allowed one of the medics to help her to the truck's bumper where she could sit.

As the medics saw to Caitlin and Karl Fletcher, more police and sheriff deputies arrived to take everyone's statements. As two of the main players in the altercation, the first thing the cops did was separate Bodie from Caitlin. But Bodie did his best to keep her in sight.

He never wanted to let her out of his sight again. Bodie acknowledged the fact that he didn't care that the immediate threat to her was now in custody. He needed to know she was safe always. And happy. He desperately wanted to make her happy.

But did his need come from the same part of his brain

that had needed to take risks? The part of his brain he'd sworn to stop listening to?

As he watched her act out the kidnapping attempt for the police as best she could while seated on the truck's bumper, Bodie realized the answer to the question was a resounding *no*. Because his need to protect her and make her happy for the rest of her life came from his heart.

He hadn't simply fallen hard for Caitlin. He was in love with her. She'd captured his heart the second he'd looked down at her from atop Dutch and fallen into her beautiful eyes. And that blue tear she'd painted at the corner of one of those eyes. She'd had him at the sight of that blue tear.

"Bodie!" Danny hollered at him as he and Cabe, who had a rolled-up towel in one hand, ran toward him. "What happened? We heard you were in a fight." Danny's eyes were wide as he took in the scene, now swarming with law enforcement and rodeo personnel. An ambulance pulled up at the opposite end of the row of livestock trailers.

Bodie tilted his hat toward the thieving, murderous rat bastard the cops were now leading to the back of the ambulance. Bodie *had* broken the guy's ribs.

Good.

"There's our bad guy. I caught him trying to shove Caitlin into his truck."

"And you sent him to the hospital?" Cabe asked with a huge grin.

Bodie noticed his knees were covered in dust and slapped at his jeans. "It seems if I hadn't taken up bull riding as a kid, I could have had a future in football."

"Or law enforcement," the police officer who had been taking his statement interjected without looking up from her notepad.

Danny snorted.

Cabe said, "Speaking of which…" He held out the towel to the police officer, opening it up. It wasn't simply a rolled-up towel. The towel was covering a cattle prod. "We found this inside our horse trailer."

The police officer looked up from her notepad with her eyebrows raised.

Bodie said, "Both of the bulls set loose on Caitlin had been shocked—"

"Viciously," Cabe interjected.

Bodie agreed, "Yes, they'd been shocked viciously with a cattle prod. Probably that cattle prod."

The officer reached for the prod. "You said you found it in your horse trailer?"

Danny said, "Yes. But we don't use those."

"I don't even own one," Bodie said.

Cabe pointed at the prod. "He was obviously trying to pin it on us if he succeeded."

The officer wrapped the prod back up. "Thanks guys." To Bodie she said, "We'll be in touch."

He tugged the brim of his hat. "No problem."

Garrett approached them. "Will someone please tell me what is going on here?"

Bodie looked to Cabe, who sent him an *I got it* nod. Cabe intercepted Garrett and redirected him toward the bull pens.

Danny asked him, "Now what?"

Bodie found Caitlin again, now surrounded by her friend Amanda and members of her family. "I have a princess to win."

CAITLIN TRIED TO keep track of where Bodie was while the police officer interviewed him. She desperately wanted to tell him what she'd learned from her grandfather about why her family had been conditioned to hate his.

And she wanted, no *needed*, him to acknowledge that he wasn't to blame for Charlie's death.

But it seemed every person who heard what had happened to her wanted a recounting directly from her. Amanda, in particular, wouldn't believe Caitlin was really unharmed.

When Caitlin looked back to where she'd last seen Bodie speaking with a police officer and Danny and Cabe, he was gone. A much different kind of panic zinged through her. She still needed to tell him what she'd learned. To thank him again for saving her. To tell him how she felt.

That she loved him.

A gentle hand settled on her shoulder.

She turned. Bodie stood next to her, his gaze molten steel.

He watched the medic finish securing the end of the elastic bandage wrapped around her instep and ankle then asked, "How is it?"

"She sprained it pretty good, but nothing ice and rest won't cure."

"No bullfighting?"

The medic snorted as he closed up his bag. "Definitely no bullfighting. At least for a couple of weeks."

Bodie met Caitlin's gaze, probably expecting outrage, but she wasn't sure how she felt about not being able to fulfill her promise, or if she even intended to do so now. Knowing that her mother hadn't been in her right mind when she'd extracted the promise lifted a huge burden from Caitlin's shoulders. She still intended to face her fear of bulls, but maybe she'd be better off doing it by helping Bodie with his bulls. If he'd have her.

Caitlin beckoned Amanda close and whispered, "Cover for me, okay?"

Amanda frowned at her, but said, "Yeah, sure. Of course."

Caitlin squeezed her friend's arm in thanks then gathered up her sock and boot and raised a hand to Bodie so he could help her stand.

He slipped one arm behind her and the other beneath her legs and picked her up completely instead. "Where to, ma'am?"

Caitlin looked at the cluster of Amanda, Ian, Liam, and Red, then back to Bodie. "Some place we can talk."

"You got it." He turned and carried her away.

Behind her, Caitlin heard Ian say, "Where's she going?"

Amanda answered, "The restroom." The girl was fast on her feet, for sure.

Caitlin wrapped her arms around his neck and held on tight. The moment she buried her face in the crook of his neck and breathed in his spicy masculine scent, all the terror she'd felt when that awful man grabbed her, and the adrenaline that had fueled her resistance, poured out of her. She burst into tears.

Bodie slowed and tried to pull back enough to see her face, but she simply tightened her hold around his neck. He said, "I knew it, you're hurt worse than a sprained ankle."

She vigorously shook her head against his neck and shoulder. "No," she sniffled. "I'm not hurt. He just scared me."

Bodie kissed her hair. "It's okay. You're okay. I've got you. I've got you now." He hitched her higher against his chest as he carried her in the direction of his fifth wheel.

"But did you hear what he said? What he said about my mom?"

"I did, sweetheart. I'm so sorry."

She pulled back and looked up into his handsome face that was already so dear to her. "And you! He could have killed you, too, when he was trying to hurt Charlie."

Bodie ran his thumb along her side. "But he didn't. I survived."

"And you're not to blame for what happened. Everyone will know that now."

Bodie lifted one shoulder in a half-shrug. "I'm still the one who turned his back on a bull everyone warned me about to whoop it up over an eight second ride, Caitlin."

"But he would have been just another rank bull if that

guy hadn't done something to him."

Another shrug.

Caitlin blew out a breath in frustration over Bodie's insistence on taking the blame for his wreck. When they reached his trailer, she loosened her hold on his neck so he could set her on her good foot while he opened the trailer door. He reached to pick her up again, but she waved him off and hopped up the steps on her own. He held on to her waist to steady her.

Hopping to the dinette and sitting down, she continued, "I found out something else after you left my family's trailer earlier." She used the sleeve of her shirt to wipe at her face. He reached into his back pocket and produced a red and black bandana neatly folded into a square. He handed it to her with the sweetest smile. She nearly burst into tears again. "You are such a good man, Bodie Hadley."

"I don't know about that."

"But I do. I also now know why my family has been virtually programmed to dislike your family."

Bodie filled a clean mug with water and handed it to her. "Do tell."

She took a long drink of the soothing water before she said, "My grandfather finally told us why there is this feud between our families."

"I've wondered, but no one in my family has ever been willing to talk about it." He reached into the freezer portion of the small fridge and pulled out a bag of ice, apparently a staple of those involved with bulls. "Our ranches are miles away from each other, so it can't be over water rights."

"No. It's much more basic."

"Oh yeah?" He wrapped the ice in a dish towel and gestured for her to lift her injured ankle onto the bench. She did, but he gently lifted it higher so he could slide beneath it. He settled her foot on his lap and carefully placed the ice on top of her injured ankle. His expression of concern and the care he was taking with her made her heart bump in her chest.

"It was a woman."

He looked at her and blinked. "A woman?"

"Specifically, your grandmother."

"You're kidding."

"Nope. It seems my grandfather had been together with her first, but your grandfather stole her from him."

"*Stole?*"

"His word, not mine."

Bodie's laugh was incredulous. "You are *kidding* me."

"Nope," she repeated. "He said your grandfather had stolen the love of his life, and that's why we are all supposed to hate any and all Hadleys."

Bodie grew serious. "So, do you?"

She looked into his stormy eyes. "Hate any and all Hadleys? Well, I really only know one, and I can say, unequivocally, that I do not hate him. Just the exact opposite actually."

"The exact opposite of hate being…"

He tried to make it sound teasing, but there was nothing joking about his expression.

She pulled in a deep breath and took the biggest risk of

her life, one even bigger than facing her fear of bulls. "Love, Bodie. The opposite of hate is love."

"Huh. What do you know. I happen to feel the opposite of hate for the one Neisson I know also."

Caitlin's eyes filled with tears again. Only this time, they were tears of joy.

Bodie made a strangled noise in his throat and gathered her to him, careful not to jostle her ankle. "I'm never going to let you out my sight again, Caitlin Neisson."

She half laughed, half cried. "That, Bodie Hadley, will get annoying."

He squeezed her again and nuzzled her hair. "You know what I mean. I want you in my life."

"You got it."

Because he was one bull rider who truly deserved his second chance.

EPILOGUE

CAITLIN THREW HER head back and laughed as she turned in a circle in the middle of the covered arena attached to the Wright Ranch bull barn, four three-month-old baby bulls trailing in her wake. They always seemed to think she had a milk bottle somewhere on her person. Granted, she usually did, but not at the moment. The lack didn't stop four velveteen noses from snuffling every inch of her they could reach.

It was a moment straight from her childhood. A moment she hoped to repeat for the rest of her life.

"What's all the cackling about?" her grandfather asked as he came out of his office. The smile he always tried to hide beneath his white beard said he knew exactly why she was so happy.

She grinned at him and continued to lead the babies in a tight circle. "I do not cackle."

Bodie stepped through Thomas Wright's office door. "Yeah, you kinda do."

Caitlin stopped so fast two of the calves bumped into her. The other two took the opportunity to surround her. Caitlin looked between the two men, her surprise giving way to worry. "What's going on?"

Her grandfather hitched a thumb toward Bodie. "I was just having a chat with your young man, here."

Caitlin wasn't sure what she found more shocking—that her grandfather had been having a chat with Bodie or that he'd referred to him as her young man. "About…?"

"I'll let him tell you," Grandfather said, then turned and walked back to his office, patting Bodie on the shoulder as he went by.

Caitlin could only blink at them. While Thomas Wright had refused to say more on the subject after telling them why he'd hated—and expected his family to hate—the Hadleys for so long, there had been a definite shift evident in him. Especially after he'd learned what his former ranch hand had done and how Bodie had thwarted the man's attempts to further harm their family. But the spectacle of him extending such a good-natured gesture toward Bodie nearly knocked her flat.

"Close your mouth, Cait, before you catch some flies." Bodie grinned at her as only he could and sauntered forward.

She snapped her mouth shut. "My brothers always say that."

His grin widened. "I know." He surveyed the calves still nuzzling her. "Is there room for me in your fan club?"

"I'm sure we can squeeze you in somewhere." She ruffled the curls on one baby bull's head while another one reached out an impossibly long tongue to lick her. She laughed again.

His gray eyes glowing silver, Bodie eased his way between the babies and dropped a quick kiss on her mouth. "It's good to see you so happy."

"I am happy. Thanks to you."

"You made your way back here,"—he gestured to the bull barn—"all by yourself."

She had faced her fears and reclaimed a part of her life, of herself, but would never discount the role Bodie had played. Not just by saving her life, but by believing in her.

She smiled up at him. "So are you going to tell me what you and Grandfather were *chatting* about? Should I be worried?"

Bodie slipped an arm around her waist and pulled her close to him, dislodging a very wet and curious nose from her front jeans pocket. "I hope not. I came to ask him something."

Caitlin's heart rate picked up. "Oh? What? If I may ask, that is."

"Seeing as it concerns you, yes, you may ask."

"Bodie!" She tried to swat his backside, but a calf was in the way. "Just tell me."

His mischievous grin faded away, and he reached into the breast pocket of his checked flannel shirt. "I wanted to know if I had his permission to give you this." He pulled a diamond ring out of the pocket and held it up to her between his thumb and forefinger.

Caitlin's heart thumped in her chest, and she could only stare at him again.

"He said yes, by the way." The grin returned, but there was a touch of insecurity hovering at the edges.

"Is that—"

"An engagement ring? Yes, it is. Caitlin, please say you'll make me the happiest man on earth by marrying me?"

Tears of joy springing to her eyes, Caitlin threw her arms around Bodie's neck and squeezed him tight. "Yes, Bodie. Hell yes."

THE END

If you enjoyed this book, please leave a review at your favorite online retailer! Even if it's just a sentence or two it makes all the difference.

Thanks for reading *The Bull Rider's Second Chance* by Leah Vale!

Discover your next romance at TulePublishing.com.

TULE
PUBLISHING

If you enjoyed *The Bull Rider's Second Chance,*
you'll love the next book in....

THE RODEO ROMEOS SERIES

Book 1: *The Bull Rider's Second Chance*

Book 2
Coming soon!

Available now at your favorite online retailer!

If you enjoyed *The Bull Rider's Second Chance*, you'll love Tule's upcoming cowboy books!

The Rancher's Proposal
by Paula Altenburg

The Cowboy's Hunt
by Jamie K. Schmidt

Coming Home to the Cowboy
by Megan Ryder

Available now at your favorite online retailer!

ABOUT THE AUTHOR

Having never met an unhappy ending she couldn't mentally "fix," Leah Vale believes writing romance novels is the perfect job for her. A Pacific Northwest native with a B.A. in Communications from the University of Washington, she lives in Central Oregon, with a huge golden retriever who thinks he's a lap dog. While having the chance to share her "happy endings from scratch" is a dream come true, dinner generally has to come premade from the store.

Thank you for reading

THE BULL RIDER'S SECOND CHANCE

If you enjoyed this book, you can find more from all our great authors at TulePublishing.com, or from your favorite online retailer.

TULE
PUBLISHING

Made in the USA
Monee, IL
29 September 2022

14901444R00135